# SUDDEN ATTRACTION

BY

*USA TODAY* Bestselling Author

REBECCA YORK

(Ruth Glick writing as Rebecca York)

All the characters in this book have no existence outside the imagination of the author, and have no relation whatsoever to anyone bearing the same name or names. They are not even distantly inspired by any individual known or unknown to the author, and all the incidents are pure invention.



First published in Great Britain 2012
by Mills & Boon, an imprint of Harlequin (UK) Limited,
Eton House, 18-24 Paradise Road, Richmond, Surrey TW9 1SR



ISBN: 978 0 263 89526 1
ebook ISBN: 978 1 408 97233 5

946-0512

Harlequin (UK) policy is to use papers that are natural, renewable and recyclable products and made from wood grown in sustainable forests. The logging and manufacturing processes conform to the legal environmental regulations of the country of origin.

Printed and bound in Spain
by Blackprint CPI, Barcelona

Award-winning, *USA TODAY* bestselling novelist Ruth Glick, who writes as **Rebecca York**, is the author of more than one hundred books, including her popular 43 LIGHT STREET series for Mills & Boon® Intrigue. Ruth says she has the best job in the world. Not only does she get paid for telling stories, she's also the author of twelve cookbooks. Ruth and her husband, Norman, travel frequently, researching locales for her novels and searching out new dishes for her cookbooks.

# *Chapter One*

While Gabriella Boudreaux filled a tray of chocolate eclairs with pastry cream in the kitchen of Chez Emile, she was fighting off panic. When the phone rang, she knew it was for her. With bad news.

As one of the prep staff called her name, she put down the pastry bag she was holding, wiped her hands on her white apron and crossed the kitchen.

The anxious voice on the other end of the line belonged to her mother.

"Gabriella, you've got to come home."

"Mom, we've talked about this before. I'm in the middle of getting ready for the evening rush. I can't drop everything and drive to Lafayette."

"You have to!"

"What's wrong?"

"There's a man stalking me."

Gabriella's hand clamped on the receiver. Over the past few years, she watched and worried as she'd seen her mother's mental state deteriorating. There had been too many instances when Gabriella had hurried home to take care of some emergency or another—only to have her mother ask why she was there.

"I can't leave right now," she said. "I have to work."

"I need you."

The mom's pleading tone almost undid her, but she managed to say, "Can you get Paula to help you out?"

The voice on the other end of the line turned petulant. "I don't want Paula."

"She's your best friend. I'll come home as soon as I can get away," she answered, thinking that she'd have to spend the night in Lafayette, then rush back to New Orleans to start work again in the morning.

When her mother started crying, Gabriella's heart squeezed painfully. "Mom, I'm sorry. Truly. I'll be there in a few hours."

"That will be too late."

She looked up and saw Emile Gautreaux watching her. A short, plump man with thinning gray hair, he had been a darling of the New Orleans restaurant scene for more than thirty years. When arthritis and his increasing bulk had curtailed his ability to function efficiently, he had hired several surrogates to populate his kitchen. Gabriella was the senior pastry chef.

"I've got to go. I'll see you later," she said into the phone.

Her mother's high-pitched voice still rang over the line as she replaced the receiver in the cradle. Dropping her hand, she took a moment to compose herself before looking up at the man who treated his professional staff like plantation hands.

He was still eyeing her. "Something wrong, chère?" he asked in the deep bayou accent that his customers found so appealing.

"No. Everything is fine."

"I hope there is not going to be a problem," he replied with the edge in his voice that he only used with staff.

"I'll handle it."

"I hope so." He gave a curt nod. When he strode over to

the stove to taste the shrimp and andouille gumbo simmering in a large pot, she let out the breath she was holding.

She wanted to make her mark in the food world, and despite Emile's slave driver attitude, he'd provided her with a wonderful chance to showcase her work. She'd received some glowing reviews in the local papers, on food blogs and even one of the airline magazines, but she'd started to wonder if she could have a life and work for Gautreaux at the same time.

She longed to tell him she had to take some personal time this afternoon, but it wouldn't do her or Mom any good if she got fired and had to look for another job.

She finished the eclairs on automatic pilot, cataloguing her own shortcomings as she worked.

She'd never been the daughter her mother wanted, and Mom had never let her forget it. Which left her feeling more on edge than ever.

Janie Rivers glided over. Janie was also working as a pastry chef at Chez Emile—under Gabriella's direction—and Gabriella's intuition told her that the other woman was looking for an opportunity to move up in the food chain.

"Did you get a complaint about one of your desserts?"

"No," Gabriella snapped. Then softened her voice. "A problem at home."

"I'm so sorry."

Yeah, I'll bet, Gabriella thought, but there was no point in saying it aloud.

"What can I do to help?" Janie asked.

"I've finished the eclairs, the chocolate torte and the flourless chocolate cake. I've still got to do the lemon sponge, the cinnamon ice cream that goes with the torte and the peach crisp."

"I can do the ice cream."

Despite her previous thought about Janie's career ambitions, Gabriella gave her a grateful smile. "I'll owe you one."

"Oh, don't worry about it. We all help each other out when we can."

When Janie reached out to touch Gabriella's shoulder, she automatically took a step back, and the other woman dropped her hand.

As long as she could remember, Gabriella hadn't liked being touched. She couldn't explain the aversion. She only knew that it usually made her nerves jangle.

"Got to get started on the lemon sponge." Quickly Gabriella went to the storage bin where the restaurant kept the flour, then brought out lemons, eggs and sugar.

Ordering herself to focus on her work so she could finish up and get out of here, she began grating lemon peel.

But she couldn't shake the worry that something was different at home this time. Something bad was going to happen, and she was going to be too late.

There was no way to explain the feeling. It might simply have come from guilt or from the abilities that she'd developed in her teens. It wasn't anything that she could explain—or wanted to talk about, to be frank. But sometimes she caught a glimmer of the future.

Like when little Billy Poirier had wandered into the bayou, and she was sure he wasn't going to be found alive. Or maybe that had been her fear—not her foreknowledge. Because there was no way to prove it either way.

By the time she packed up some of yesterday's desserts for Mom and left Chez Emile, it was already late in the afternoon and rush-hour traffic on I-10 was brutal. As she sat in the car, gripping the steering wheel, her sense of anxiety grew.

Drivers weren't supposed to talk on the phone without a

headset, which she didn't have. Nevertheless, she punched in her mom's number and listened to the phone ring.

When she heard her mother's voice, her heart leaped, but it was only the answering machine asking her to leave a message.

"Mom, I'm on my way. I'll be there as soon as I can."

Her stomach was in knots now. Three hours later, when she finally reached the turnoff to the plantation where she'd grown up, she breathed out a small sigh.

If you didn't know much about the Boudreaux family, you might think they were well off.

Her mother still lived in the nineteenth-century mansion she'd inherited from her parents, but she'd abandoned the whole second floor to save on utilities, and she supplemented her income by renting out furnished cottages on the property. Still, when Gabriella had suggested selling off some of the acreage, her mother had refused.

Mom's car was in the circular drive in front of the mansion, but another vehicle was pulled up, too.

As Gabriella cut the engine, her mother's friend Paula Aucoin came rushing down the steps. The expression on her face was a confirmation of Gabriella's worst fears.

"What is it? What's wrong?"

"Honey, I'm so sorry. There's been an accident."

Her throat clenched, but she managed to say, "It's bad, right?"

"It looks like Marian fell down the steps. I'm sorry. She's dead."

Gabriella struggled to take that in. "But...but she never goes upstairs."

"I know. That's why it's so strange. She was worried about something, and she called me. When I got here, she was sprawled at the bottom of the steps, unconscious."

Gabriella gasped. "She called me. I...I couldn't leave

the restaurant. I…" Her voice trailed off as terrible guilt assaulted her. "She wanted me to come home."

"It wouldn't have done any good. I think she called me right after she talked to you, and I came straight over. I'm right here in town, but when I got here, she had already fallen."

Gabriella nodded numbly. The explanation didn't help. All she knew was that she should have dropped everything and come home.

"Where is she now?"

"The LeBlanc Funeral Home. She'd written me a letter about what she wanted to happen after she died."

Gabriella swallowed hard, thinking that she should have been the one to get the letter. But Mom had relied on Paula more than her own daughter.

"Come in. Sit down and have a cup of coffee."

She was torn. She should go to the funeral home, but she sensed that Paula wanted to talk to her, so she allowed the older woman to take her into the kitchen. It was at the back of the house, and the breakfast room looked out over weedy gardens and a slow-moving bayou.

She stood for a moment, breathing in the familiar scents. Fried bacon. Strong Cajun coffee. This was where her love of cooking had been born. First she'd helped with mixing batter and stirring soup. Then she'd started following recipes on her own. Her relationship with Mom might have been troubled, but the kitchen was one place where they had connected.

When Gabriella walked to the coffeemaker on the worn Formica counter, Paula waved her toward the table. "Sit down. I know you've had a bad shock."

"So have you."

"I've had some time to absorb it." Paula got down mugs and poured two cups of the strong coffee that Mom must have made that morning.

"Your mother was so proud of you."

Gabriella looked up in surprise. "She was?"

"Yes. She'd talk about your career all the time. About how the famous Emile Gautreaux relied on you."

"She didn't say that to me."

"It was hard for her to…reach out to you."

"Why?" Gabriella asked, curious to get Paula's take on their relationship.

"When your father was sick, she wanted to spend as much time with him as she could. After he died, she felt like she'd lost her connection with you."

Gabriella had been only three years old when her father had been diagnosed with stomach cancer, and her mom had thrown herself into nursing him. When he'd died a couple of years after that, Gabriella had felt as if her mother was a stranger, and they'd never been able to reach across the breach.

"She considered herself a failure for not being closer to you," Paula said.

Gabriella raised her head in shock. "But I always thought that was my fault."

"I guess Marian had the same feelings. Too bad the two of you didn't communicate better."

"I…"

"I'm not blaming you, child. It was on her as much as on you. Maybe more. The adult is the one who's supposed to take the lead."

Paula brought two mugs of coffee to the table, both with cream and sugar. When she sat down and stirred her coffee, Gabriella had the feeling there was more she was going to say.

"What is it?" she asked.

"A couple of months ago, your mom rented the Cypress Cottage to a man named Luke Buckley."

"Yes, she mentioned that. She was glad of the extra income. He wasn't any trouble, was he?"

"You mean complaining about stuff? I don't think so. But I think she regretted having him on the property."

"Why?"

"I think she was afraid of him."

"Why?" she asked again.

"She said he was secretive. I tried to tell her that maybe he just wanted to keep to himself. He could have lost his job or his wife for all we knew. Who can say why a man moves into an isolated cottage in a new location?"

"Because he's hiding from the law?" Gabriella asked, putting a different spin on the speculations.

"I don't know, but I do know she kept going on about him. He was stony. Aloof. Abrupt. He was always in there working on the computer. And there were papers scattered all over the place. When she'd come in, he'd hide them."

"Hide them?"

"Well, gather them up. And there was something about him that she just didn't trust."

"Did he have a lease?"

"I don't know. Maybe she thought he was all right at the beginning. Or…you know…she was…"

Paula let the sentence trail off, and Gabriella was sure her mother's friend was referring to her recent mental problems, although she wasn't willing to come out and say it.

Gabriella glanced out the window toward the Cypress Cottage. "Should I be worried?" she asked.

"I don't know. But you might want to watch out for him while you're here. You know, keep the doors locked."

"If he's so much of a loner, I probably won't run into him."

"Maybe, but you'll have to deal with him eventually. I mean, now he's renting from you."

Gabriella nodded, realizing that she'd inherited this property and would have to decide what to do with it.

"How long are you staying here?"

"Just a few days."

"Your mom would want you to get back to your career."

Gabriella made a soft sound. Her career. She'd made it the most important thing in her life. Until today.

If it wasn't for her ambitions, she might have stayed home, but then what? Work as a short-order cook in Lafayette? That wasn't why she'd gone to the Culinary Institute of America in New York state, then come back to Louisiana to look for a job in the best restaurants in New Orleans. Creating wonderful food gave her a satisfaction nothing else did. Or it had.

"I'd better get to the funeral home," she murmured.

"Your mom didn't want to be a burden to you, so she had everything spelled out—before..." Again Paula stopped.

"But I'm going over there anyway." Gabriella stood and carried her coffee mug to the sink. "Thank you for being here."

"Just tell me if you need anything."

"Thanks. I will."

BEING CAREFUL NOT TO STEP ON anything that would make a crunching noise, the man watching from the shadows of the trees saw Gabriella Boudreaux hurry back to her car. Probably going to the funeral home.

He waited another minute for the other woman to get into her vehicle. When they had both driven away, he made a satisfied sound.

With the two of them gone, he could finally have a smoke. He was starving for one. After quickly using his pocket lighter, he took a deep drag on the fag, grateful for the nicotine rush. He'd broken the habit out of necessity in prison. As soon as he'd gotten out, he'd started again.

While he smoked, he reviewed the day's events. The old lady had darted upstairs, and he'd followed, knowing that if he pushed her down, the daughter would come running home.

He was an expert at digging into people's backgrounds, and he knew that she was one of the children from the Solomon Clinic in Houma.

It had been set up to help infertile couples conceive children, but that was only a cover for something else. The guy who'd hired him had wanted to know what had happened there. Not the covert purpose, the unintended consequences.

The doctor had kept records of his activities, of course, but those had been destroyed in a fire long ago.

A few people in Houma had talked to him about the clinic. Which was how he'd gotten Marian Boudreaux's name.

She'd been a good place to start, but his real objectives were the children, like Gabriella. She was the one he really wanted, out here in the country, where there was more privacy and little chance of her screams being heard.

# *Chapter Two*

Gabriella was already wiped out by the time she met with Burt LeBlanc from the funeral home.

He'd gone to high school with her, although they hadn't known each other well. She hadn't been really close to anyone, except one girl named Julie Monroe. It was as if she and Julie were on the same wavelength, although she wasn't sure what that meant exactly. They'd spent time together, until Julie had moved away in their sophomore year, leaving Gabriella feeling more alone than ever. Because she'd never been great at making friends, it had been easier to keep to herself than to try and work her way into any of the established groups.

Burt LeBlanc, who'd inherited the business from his dad, greeted her as if they'd been buddies.

She shook his hand, getting through the physical contact the same way she was getting through everything else.

"I'm sorry for your loss," he said in the deep, reassuring voice that he must have cultivated.

"Yes—thanks."

"Sit down. Make yourself comfortable." He gestured toward one of the padded leather chairs across from his broad desk. "Can I get you anything? Coffee? Tea?"

"No, thanks," she answered as she lowered herself into one of the chairs.

"I read about your pastry chef career in that airline magazine."

She blinked. "You did?"

"Yes. Very impressive. People in town were talking about it."

Again, she was surprised that anybody in Lafayette would take notice of her.

After relaxing her with a little more small talk, Burt addressed the arrangements that her mom had spelled out—in an envelope full of instructions that she'd given him several years earlier.

"Your mom wished to be cremated, like your dad," he said. "There's a place waiting for her in the columbarium, next to him."

The columbarium was a building with rows of little vaults along the walls. Putting Mom next to Dad made sense, particularly because it appeared that the space was already bought and paid for.

"All right."

Burt consulted some papers on his desk. "And, of course, there's to be no viewing and no funeral."

Gabriella stared at him as she struggled to take that in. "What?"

He tapped one of the papers. "She didn't tell you that she specified a memorial service—six weeks after her death?"

"No. Did she say why?"

"She wanted the shock of her death over, and..." He paused for a moment. "And she felt it would be less expensive. The lead time would give you a chance to prepare some of the food yourself if you wanted to. She thought you could make some of those pecan pies she loved."

"Uh, yes."

Lord, Mom had certainly gotten into micromanaging the event.

Gabriella left the funeral home feeling light-headed. She'd braced to deal with her mother's friends. Now she had plenty of time to get ready for the service. And to plan what she wanted to say.

Her mother always had been detail oriented. She must have obsessed over all this before she started losing her grip. Or had she already felt her mental state deteriorating, and she'd hurried to write down these instructions while she could still think clearly?

Gabriclla made a small sound as she realized the implications of Mom's carefully considered list with its wealth of details. Her mother had been forced to deal with a daughter who didn't always follow the parental script. In death, she had the upper hand—at last.

BY THE TIME GABRIELLA returned to the plantation house, it was after sunset. The gathering darkness contributed to her feeling of being utterly alone. Neither Mom nor Dad had brothers or sisters. Which meant no aunts and uncles or cousins. It had been a small family, and it would die with her because she wasn't going to get married and have children.

Did that make her feel sad? Or relieved? She was too off balance to know.

Glad that she had left some lights on in the house, she hurried up the steps to the front door. But walking into the hall was like a sudden shock to her already frazzled nerves.

When she'd come through here with Paula, she'd been focused on her mom's friend. This time she was alone, and when she stood looking up the steps, an inexplicable feeling of terror swept over her, making her reach out and brace her hand against the wall as she struggled to catch her breath—and scrambled to make sense of what she was feeling.

Her mother had fallen here. The impact of Mom's death was hitting her again, which was why her temples were suddenly pounding. However, she knew deep down that her attack of nerves wasn't just from the accident.

Paula had said her mom had climbed the steps and fallen. But why had she gone up? To get something? Or to run away from someone? Or both?

Gabriella couldn't shove away the notion that another person had been here and something evil had happened in this hallway.

Her speculations immediately went to the tenant—Luke Buckley. Mom had been afraid of him. What if he'd come over here and attacked her?

But why?

Maybe he didn't have the rent money. They'd gotten into an argument, and he'd killed her…

"Stop it," she muttered to herself. "You're just letting your speculations run wild because this is the worst day of your life."

She clenched her fists, sure that Mom's sudden death and her own feelings of guilt were making her jump at shadows.

What did she really believe? Nothing she could prove. Not without some evidence. If she went upstairs, would she find anything suspicious? Or was there something incriminating in Cypress Cottage?

She gritted her teeth as she imagined herself spying on Luke Buckley. What if one of Mom's friends caught her doing it? People in Lafayette already thought she was a little off. Which was one of the reasons she'd known she didn't want to stay in town once she had graduated from high school.

She'd fled her childhood reputation for being weird by going across the country to culinary school then moving to New Orleans, and she didn't want it back.

But nobody was here to observe her now. Could she start with some kind of psychic impression of what had really happened in the hall—then back it up with evidence? She focused her attention on the stairs, trying to bring the past few hours into focus. Mom had been here. She'd fallen to her death, but had she been alone?

Gabriella put everything she had into trying to bring back the scene. Even as she focused on her mother in the hall—with *someone,* she silently wondered if she was sending herself on a fool's errand. No matter how much you wanted to, you couldn't see the past. Could you?

She'd never tried anything like that before, but she sensed that the scene was hovering almost within her grasp. Shadowy figures flickered at the edge of her vision. Her mom and a man?

She closed her eyes, straining to bring the vision into focus. Yes, she saw her mom, a look of fear on her face as she rushed up the stairs, trying to get away from the stalker. Gabriella saw him only from the back. Or was she making it all up?

Probably.

Struggling with frustration, she tried to see his image from a different angle. Maybe she could have done it, but a massive bolt of lightning struck nearby, so bright that she saw it through her closed eyelids.

It was followed by a clap of thunder that shook the house.

As the thunder rumbled, the lights flickered out, plunging Gabriella into inky, disorienting blackness.

She pressed her back against the wall, suddenly alarmed by the darkness, just like when she'd been little and Mom had insisted on turning out the lights at bedtime. At night, she'd always imagined ghosts from the past coming back to claim this house. Even the toys on her shelves took on sinister shapes, and the closet door had to be closed before she could even think about sleep.

In adulthood, she'd talked herself out of those juvenile

fears. But in her fragile emotional state, the sum of her childhood terrors came rushing back to her as she stood in the darkened hallway.

"Stop being ridiculous," she ordered herself. "The lights are just out. There's no bogeyman lurking around the corner."

But she couldn't deny why she'd come here in the first place. Mom had called her in a panic, talking about a stalker, and there was a man living right on the plantation property who could be up to no good.

With her heart pounding, she waited for her eyes to adjust to the dark. The moon was up, and a small amount of light came through the windows on either side of the door.

When she could see well enough, she crossed the hall and turned the lock on the door. Then she started for the kitchen to get the flashlight that Mom kept in the utility drawer.

Was there anything she could use for a weapon?

They'd never kept a gun in the house, but maybe she should have something with her, like a hammer.

SHE MADE IT TO THE KITCHEN as fast as she could in the dark and opened the utility drawer. The flashlight was there, but when she tried to click it on, the batteries were almost dead. Only a feeble light came from the bulb, and she clenched her fist on the shaft, then shut it off again. All it would do would tell someone where she was, not light her way.

Now what?

Go up to her old room? Or was it better to get out of this house, where she already felt spooked?

Luke Buckley was living in Cypress Cottage. But there were two others on the grounds. Water Iris was the closest. She'd feel more secure spending the night over there than here.

Wishing she could see what she was doing, she fumbled through another drawer and found the wad of spare keys that Mom kept. In the dark, she couldn't even be sure they were the right ones, but that was the best she could do at the moment.

After slipping the set into her purse, she headed for the back door. On the porch, she looked toward the cottages, barely making out their shapes in the darkness. Water Iris was on the extreme right. Cypress was on the left. And Crepe Myrtle was between them. That would put some space between her and Buckley.

All were blacked out, and she couldn't even discern the shape of a car parked in front of Cypress. Maybe Luke Buckley was away. Or sitting in the dark plotting murder? He'd taken care of the mother, and now he would finish off the daughter.

Acknowledging that her fears were making it difficult to think rationally, she descended the steps, then headed across the yard to the cottage. It hadn't started raining yet, but the wind was blowing the trees, sending leaves flying across the lawn.

In Gabriella's long ago memories, the grass had been well tended by a gardening company that did yard work in town. Mom had given up that service after Dad had died. For a few years, she'd tried to keep up the grounds around the house herself. But that had gone by the wayside, too, and now the grass was choked by weeds and needed mowing. She stumbled several times into what had formerly been flower beds, then finally made it to the cottages. But as she approached Water Iris, she had the sensation that someone was stalking her—like they'd been stalking Mom.

She started running, but before she'd gotten more than a few yards, a figure sprang out of the darkness at the side of Crepe Myrtle, grabbing her and pulling her to the ground.

A scream rose in her throat. Before it reached her lips, it choked off as large hands grabbed her throat. A man's hands.

At his touch, a confusing welter of impressions and sensations assaulted her.

# *Chapter Three*

In a blinding instant, Luke Buckley knew he had made a terrible mistake. In the darkness, he'd seen a shadowy figure sneaking across the lawn and been sure it was a Mafia hitman sent to murder him.

Instead, it was Gabriella Boudreaux, who had as much right to be here as he did.

But he hadn't known who she was until he'd pulled her to the ground. He loosened his hands from her neck, intending to let her go and apologize.

Except that he couldn't take his hands off her. And he couldn't put any coherent words together. Not yet. Because in the moment of grabbing on to her, something strange happened. Her mind had opened to him in a way that knocked the breath from his lungs and made his heart start to pound.

At least he was able to open his fingers and make the hands that had gripped her neck move to her shoulders.

"Sorry," he managed to whisper. Or had he even spoken the apology aloud?

His head swam as her memories leaped into his mind.

He saw her as a little girl being scolded for making a mess in the kitchen by a younger version of the woman who had rented him the Cypress Cottage. He saw her in high school squirming away when a boy crowded her into her open locker and tried to corner her there. Wandering alone into the bayou and sitting on a fallen log to get away from a town where she had never felt comfortable. Then later, more satisfied with her life, taking culinary courses and icing a chocolate cake.

Overlaying it all were the most recent, sharpest memory and the emotions swirling around it. Her coming home to discover that her mother was dead.

He cursed under his breath, feeling her pain and also her confusion at what was happening between them now.

As her memories assaulted him, his own memories were streaming into her mind. Especially one particularly vivid scene.

The reason why he was on the run.

Three months ago, he'd been at his computer, working on the book that had gotten him into so much trouble.

He'd heard a noise and turned to see a man with a gun standing in the doorway of his little office.

"You're finished with that writing project," the man growled. "Get up."

Luke got up slowly, reaching under his desk for the fire extinguisher he kept there. As he straightened, he pulled the trigger, spraying the man in the face. The guy choked and clawed at his eyes. Luke lunged forward and clunked the heavy canister down on the man's skull.

When the assailant went still, Luke reached for the phone cord and used it to tie the man's hands behind his back. Then he wound packing tape around his ankles and reinforced the phone cord with more tape.

By the time the guy's eyes blinked open, Luke was holding the gun.

"Rudy Maglioni sent you?" he growled.

The assailant sneered. "Like I'm going to tell you."

"What happens when you have to go back to him and explain that you failed? Or will you have to skip town?"

The only answer was a string of curses.

Luke grabbed the man's hair, yanking his head up and using more masking tape to gag him. His heart was pounding, but he began methodically gathering up the papers on his desk.

He unplugged his laptop, took an already packed duffel bag from the closet and walked out of the room, forcing himself not to run when he wanted to dash to his car.

His attention was brought back to the present as he heard Gabriella gasp.

With the memories—his and hers—came physical sensations that walked a line between pain and pleasure. He scrambled to explain it to himself and could come up with nothing beyond the violence of the encounter.

"Gabriella."

In the darkness, he couldn't see her face, but he didn't need sight to know what she looked like. Dark-blond hair cut short. Light eyes. A delicate nose. Tempting lips that drew him with an intensity he had never felt before—much less imagined. He lowered his head, and as his mouth touched hers, he was caught by a blaze of need that radiated to every cell of his body.

They had just met. Met? Not exactly. In his haste to protect himself from another mob attack, he had struck first without knowing who she was.

Yet they'd gone from strangers to intimates in seconds. Without understanding why it had happened, he wanted her. Right here. Right now. Out in the open.

And she wanted him. He knew it by the way her lips moved over his and by the desire reverberating through her mind. Those signals were as clear to him as their shared memories.

He gathered her close, rocking on the weedy grass, frustrated by the layers of clothing separating them. He wanted her naked. In a bed. This would have to do.

Those heated thoughts and the pain pounding through his brain almost wiped out his ability to think, but not quite. Somewhere in his consciousness, he understood that what they were doing was dangerous. That knowledge was as sharp and insistent as the desire binding them together. And the pain in his head.

And she understood, too. He felt her wrench her mouth away, felt her push at his shoulder to free herself.

"No," she gasped. "We can't."

Strange as it sounded, in that frantic moment, he knew he had come close to having his brain explode.

Oh, come on!

Even as he dismissed that notion, he rolled away from her, panting, his head spinning. Still, he was as aware of her as he was of himself. He heard her breath coming fast and sharp. Felt the beating of her heart, although that should be impossible.

He couldn't label what had happened. Not the psychic… exchange of information. Or the swell of desire. Or the conviction that they skated on the edge of disaster.

Not yet. Maybe never. He was too shaken by the whole encounter. And the worst part was that he knew what she always struggled to conceal—how alone she felt. And she knew the same thing about him.

Both of them had learned to bury that innermost truth but not when someone had invaded your mind.

Invasion? Was that the right word? What the hell had happened?

She broke into his thoughts, speaking in a shaky voice.

"Luke Buckley," she said. They were meeting for the first time, but she knew his name. "The man who rented Cypress Cottage."

"Yes," he answered, knowing her mom could have told her that much. But that didn't account for her absolute conviction that it was him.

And, unfortunately, she zeroed in on a fact that he needed to keep hidden. "That's not your real name. You're…"

"Don't say it."

"Why?"

"You know why."

He clenched his teeth. The whole situation was so damned weird that he wanted to shout a string of curses, if that wouldn't have made things worse.

This wasn't the way he would have wanted to meet *anyone*. Particularly not this woman who—what? Who had connected with him in ways that he still could hardly believe.

He heard himself say, "We have to talk."

He was sure she wanted to refuse, for a whole host of reasons, starting with the way he'd thrown her to the ground, but she answered with a small sound that signaled acquiescence.

The wind had picked up, and a few fat drops of rain began to fall.

"We'd better get inside before it starts to pour. Come to my cottage."

She dragged in a breath. "You've got to be kidding. You just attacked me on my own property."

"And you know why," he said again.

He understood she was still making up her mind as more drops plopped down.

"You left the plantation house," he said. "Because you were afraid to be there alone in the dark."

She didn't bother denying it or asking how he knew. It was the same way she knew that he'd changed his name when he fled to Lafayette, Louisiana.

"I was going to Water Iris, not to you," she answered in a strained voice.

"You might as well come to Cypress. I've got some battery lights."

She looked toward his cottage. "They're not on."

"They can be."

Luke waited while Gabriella made up her mind. He knew she had to be going over the scene between them. His throwing her to the ground and fastening his hands around her neck. The opening of their minds to a level of intimacy that should have been impossible. The pressure building inside each of their heads. And the sexual need that had overwhelmed them.

That might turn out to be the final factor that sent her running from him. But perhaps she was pretending it hadn't happened because she finally said, "All right."

Wordlessly, he started for Cypress, and she followed a few paces behind him.

FROM THE SHADOWS, George Camden watched and listened, his hands clenched as he cursed the way his excellent plans had just gotten screwed up.

When he'd heard the thunder, he'd thought the storm would give him some cover when he broke into the mansion again so he could grab Gabriella. Then he'd watched her come out of the house and thought, what luck.

He'd been on his way toward her when Luke Buckley had tackled her. There was something strange about him, although George hadn't figured it out yet. But it looked as if the guy had started to assault her, then changed his mind. Yeah, assault had turned into a pretty heated scene.

He laughed. That was an interesting development.

Too bad the guy had stuck his nose in where it didn't belong.

But why?

He'd heard them talking. It had been a strange conversation, as if George was only hearing part of it. Which could have been true from the way the wind was howling. Maybe it had carried away words spoken softly, but he had caught that Luke Buckley wasn't his real name. Interesting.

Did they know each other or not? Part of the time it had sounded as if they did—then not so much.

Or maybe the mom had given the daughter an earful about the renter. Did Mrs. Boudreaux know that the guy was using an alias? Or just the daughter?

As drops of rain hit his head, George narrowed his eyes. He hadn't signed up for this job to be wet and miserable. However, Gabriella had to come out of the guy's cottage some time, and when she did, he wanted to be ready.

Lips set in a grim line, he moved cautiously across the lawn, finding a spot under a tree that gave him a little shelter—and where he could still watch the cottage door.

Of course, you weren't supposed to stand under a tree in a lightning storm, but he'd take a chance on that.

As he huddled in the cold, he played the scene again in his mind. Why had Buckley come out in the first place? Did he suspect someone else was on the property? Or was he just jumpy about something to do with his alias?

One thing was sure: renting a cottage on the plantation had put Luke Buckley in the wrong place at the wrong time—as far as George was concerned. Too bad for him.

LUKE AND GABRIELLA HURRIED onto the porch as the storm finally broke, sending rain pouring down.

"Close call," he muttered as he opened the door.

When she hung back, he stepped quickly inside and turned on two of the battery-powered lamps that he'd bought after Mrs. Boudreaux had told him the electricity often went out in the middle of a storm.

Gabriella came in after him. As she looked around at the mess he'd made of the living room, he suddenly wished that he hadn't been so quick to offer the lamps. However, if he hadn't, she might not have come inside.

He knew she was staring at the epitome of a junked-up bachelor pad. He'd been working, and he'd left papers all over the desk. Books and other research materials were stacked on the coffee and end tables. Sitting on top of them were several plates and glasses that he hadn't carried to the kitchen area, which was at the side of the room.

Of course, he hadn't expected company, but still, he should have kept the place a little neater. What if his landlady dropped by?

Well, that wasn't going to happen, he reminded himself.

He quickly picked up the glasses and plates and ferried them to the sink. Probably he should have hired a maid. But then he'd have to put his papers away. They were confidential, and dangerous, come to that.

He swept them into a pile now, putting them into a desk drawer.

He didn't want Gabriella poking around his research, for her sake as well as his. The less she knew about the New Jersey mob, the better.

Of course, she'd been poking around in his mind, he reminded himself. Which meant she already knew too much.

Turning, he said, "I'm sorry about your mother."

"Thank you. Or whatever you're supposed to say."

"That works. Why don't you sit down," he offered, thinking how lame that sounded.

Without comment, she took one of the easy chairs facing the sofa.

He leaned his hips against the kitchen counter, trying to

look as if he wasn't studying her, seeing in person what he'd only seen in his mind. Her short blond hair framed a narrow face, and her large, expressive eyes were either green or blue. She was staring back, taking his measure with as much interest. He knew his dark hair was too long and that he hadn't shaved in a couple of days. Probably he looked like a criminal. Which might be what she was already thinking.

To break the silence, he asked, "Can I get you something? A beer? I've got some from the local brewery."

She pursed her lips. "Okay. Maybe I could use one."

"Yeah, I guess you had a rough day."

"Uh-huh."

It was a strange conversation, two people who should know nothing about each other. But not really. Not when they'd suddenly gotten inside each other's heads.

Although he wanted to ask, *that mind to mind thing ever happen to you before?* he hadn't worked up the nerve yet.

He pulled out two bottles out of the refrigerator and twisted off the caps.

"Do you want a glass?"

"No, this is fine."

He moved back to the living area and set one of the bottles on the coffee table, then lowered himself to the other easy chair.

Outside the rain pounded down, giving him a feeling of two people meeting at the end of the world, like in the science fiction stories he'd read as a kid. Science fiction had appealed to him, maybe because he'd been disappointed with reality.

They each took a sip of beer.

Although he'd turned on a couple of battery lights, he thought the conversation might go better in semidarkness.

She ran her finger around the outside of the beer bottle before breaking the silence. "What happened out there?"

He winced. "I thought you were sneaking up on me."

"Lucky you didn't shoot me."

"Yeah."

"That was a gun I felt in your waistband."

"Yeah," he said again, pulling it out and setting it on the table between them.

She stared down at it and took another sip of beer before saying, "I didn't mean—why did you tackle me. I meant—what happened when we touched?"

She'd been brave enough to ask the question. All he could say was, "We read each other's thoughts and memories."

"Which should be impossible." She added, "So the next question is—how did it happen?"

He shrugged. "I don't know." The silence stretched again before he asked, "Do you have some psychic ability?"

She hesitated. "Not that you could…document."

"Which means what?"

She raised one shoulder. "It means, there were times when I got a glimpse of the future."

"Like what?"

"My mom called this afternoon. I knew it was going to be her, and I sensed that something bad…" Her voice trailed off, and she started again, "Something bad was going to happen. I didn't know she was going to…die." Her voice cracked, and he could see she was struggling not to cry.

He wanted to cross the room and put his arms around her, pull her close and stroke her back, her hair. But he stayed where he was.

When it looked as if she'd regained control, he said, "And you feel guilty about not dropping everything and coming here."

"Yes."

"But you were too far away to change what happened."

"That doesn't make it better."

He nodded.

"What about you?" she asked. "I mean have you had psychic experiences?"

He tried to answer as honestly as he could. "I'm an investigative journalist."

"Working on a book that will blow Rudy Maglioni's New Jersey mob operation wide open."

"Yeah. But let's not get sidetracked," he said in a tight voice.

"Okay."

"I always thought that I had better than average instincts for stories. Good instincts for interviews. I've got a pretty good idea when someone's lying to me. I know when I can push them to say more than they intended. I know when letting the silence stretch will make them jump to fill the vacuum."

"Useful."

"But nothing like…that thing outside has ever happened to me."

"So what was different tonight?" she pressed.

"We're both on edge. I mean, your mother just died, and I…"

"You're hiding out from the…wiseguys. You're willing to risk your life to finish the book."

"Like I said, let's drop it," he snapped. "And that doesn't explain the weird stuff."

"I guess not."

They stared at each other.

"I should leave," she said.

"I wouldn't advise it. You said you sometimes have an inkling of the future. What if you didn't want to stay in the house because of…the stalker."

"What stalker?"

"Come on. That's what your mom called about."

She sighed. "Inconvenient that you picked that up from my mind."

"Like your knowing too much about my damn book. Inconvenient."

Again, they lapsed into a tense silence.

He was used to letting the other person do the talking, but he ventured, "We picked up all that stuff from each other… when we touched."

"Yes."

He shifted in the chair. "We could try it again. See what happens."

Her posture became more guarded. "There was more than just an exchange of information," she said in a hard voice. "You wanted…me."

"It wasn't exactly one-sided. You wanted me, too."

She kept her gaze fixed on him as she asked in a hard voice, "Did you do something to me?"

"What the hell is that supposed to mean?"

"Use some kind of voodoo hex?"

"You're kidding, right?"

"Okay, maybe not voodoo. What about some kind of hypnosis technique you learned from your vast research?"

He spread his hands. "I don't have any secret techniques."

"I'm just trying to figure it out."

"We both are. And you must know I was as confounded as you by what happened." He paused a beat before asking, "Did it give you a headache?"

She stared back at him. "Yes. Did it do that to you, too?"

"Yes."

He wanted to press her for information. No, he wanted to touch her again, badly. And it was almost impossible not to act on the impulse. He pictured himself leaping out of the chair, crossing the room and pulling her into his arms. To get information?

Perhaps, but the sexual component was as strong as the need to explore the psychic link. He had touched her, kissed her, and felt an instant craving like nothing else he had ever experienced. It was as if the two of them had been born to connect.

Well, he might think that, but he didn't dare say it because he didn't want to send her running out into the night.

To cool his ardor, he asked, "Did you have trouble making friends with people?"

By the look on her face, he knew the directness of the question had caught her by surprise.

She swallowed. "You know I did. You did, too. We found that out when we touched."

No use denying it. Most people formed easy relationships. He couldn't do it because it always seemed that something was missing. Which was probably why he'd chosen his profession. If he couldn't get close to people on a personal level, he could know more about them than anybody else. Sometimes he dug up secrets that the world needed to know. Or was that putting it in terms that were too grandiose?

"If we have trouble making friends, then what happened tonight?" he challenged.

"I don't know, but we're not friends."

"What are we?"

She moistened her lips, and he had to wrench his gaze away from her mouth. It was more difficult than ever not to cross the room and wrap his arms around her. Something would happen when he did.

"Don't."

"You're reading my mind?"

"Your expression." She lifted one shoulder as she stared at him.

"I'm not going to do anything you don't want."

"Isn't that a standard male line?"

"Yeah, but in this case it's true. You could make sure I'm telling the truth by touching me."

"No, thanks."

When she stood up abruptly, he knew he had pushed the suggestion too hard.

"Stay here." The command came out more sharply than he'd intended.

"Why?"

"Someone's out there," he said in a harsh voice.

"Back to the stalker?"

"Yeah. You'd better sleep here."

"So you can…"

"Protect you."

He held his breath while she considered the advice. If she said no, he wasn't sure what he was going to do.

Another lie. He would grab her arm to stop her. And then what? Give her another peek into his private fears and longings?

"You were here most of the time. Did you see anyone sneaking around?"

"I was inside most of the time—busy working."

"But you didn't see anybody," she insisted.

"No, but in the absence of proof, I think you have to act cautiously."

"Like you did when you started writing about Rudy Maglioni?"

"Somebody has to expose him."

"Why you?"

"Because I'm willing to take the chance." He could have added that nobody besides his editor would miss him if the mob caught up with him. Changing the subject, he said, "You can have my bed."

"No, thanks." She glanced toward the couch. "I'll stay out here."

"It's not all that comfortable."

"I'll manage," she said with an edge in her voice, and he warned himself not to press his luck. She was a woman with a strong will, and he couldn't force her decision. It had to come from her.

"I'll get you a blanket." He hurried into the bedroom and glanced at the bed he hadn't made in days. Well, maybe her coming in here wasn't such a good idea.

After pulling the spare blanket from the top of the closet, he returned to the living room. He laid it on the end of the couch and stepped back. He wanted to say that they couldn't keep from touching each other forever. Sooner or later it was going to happen again.

"You're sure you'll be okay?" he asked.

"Yes. Thanks. And…" She paused again. "Thanks for watching out for me."

"It's the right thing to do," he said stiffly, then added, "You can have the bathroom first."

"Thanks."

"Your mom put an extra toothbrush in there."

"Right. She liked to keep the cottages stocked with conveniences."

"Yes. I appreciated the food in the cabinets."

They were getting into inane conversation territory again because they still had no idea how to deal with each other.

Before he said any other dumb lines—or did anything else he regretted—he made sure the front door was locked and bolted, then picked up a lamp and entered into the bedroom.

## *Chapter Four*

Outside in the darkness, George Camden gritted his teeth. Abandoning the protection of the tree, he'd crossed the weedy lawn and gotten as close as he could to the window. He'd been able to see them, but he hadn't heard a lot of what they were saying because of the damned rain.

After a half hour out there, he was wet and cold, and he needed a smoke. Bad.

He'd been all set to get his hands on Gabriella Boudreaux tonight. Apparently that wasn't going to happen. It looked as if she was spending the night in the cottage. But not in Buckley's bed, for some reason.

So why was she there if they weren't going to do anything fun?

Maybe because her mom had died today. However, if Buckley was smart, he could have comforted her and then offered more than back patting. Despite how he'd acted outside, Buckley must be too honorable for that.

George's mind circled back to the earlier question. Why was she staying there? Did Buckley think he was protecting her?

If he was, that meant they were worried about someone snooping around. Or worried about someone causing the mom's death. Or maybe she was just upset about staying alone after coming home and finding her mother had kicked the bucket.

Yeah, that made sense.

The phone in his pocket vibrated, and he jumped, then cursed under his breath.

The only guy who had this number was the Badger, the one who'd hired him to snoop around Houma and find out about the clinic.

The phone kept vibrating as he stepped far enough away from the cottage to avoid being heard.

"Yeah?" he said as he flipped it open.

"You haven't reported in," the curt voice on the other end of the line said.

"I've been busy."

"Doing what?"

"I got a lead on one of the women who was treated at the fertility clinic. I came down to Lafayette to…question her."

"And?"

He waited a beat before admitting, "She's dead."

The curse on the other end of the line had him holding the phone away from his ear.

"I haven't heard about any murders in the news."

"Because it wasn't murder. She fell down the stairs," he said, stretching the facts. "An old lady tripping and falling isn't news."

Again, he waited through a string of curses.

"But she led me to her daughter," he said, putting the best spin he could on the past few hours.

"What's the daughter's name?"

"Gabriella Boudreaux."

"And you're going to pick her up?"

"She's with a guy."

"Who?"

"Someone named Luke Buckley. He rented a cottage on her mom's property."

"I'm paying you good money to get results."

"I will."

"If the Luke Buckley guy interferes, kill him."

Even though he'd already thought of that, he snapped, "So now you're saying you want the police investigating a murder?"

"Make sure it looks like an accident."

"If I can."

"You'd better."

The line went dead, leaving George wondering what would happen to *him* if he didn't fulfill this assignment. Would he be scheduled for an accident? Or would he just disappear?

In the bedroom, Luke put out the light and looked out the window. He couldn't see much in the darkness, but he couldn't shake the feeling that someone *was* out there in the night. Someone who shouldn't be on the property.

He was torn between slipping out the back door to investigate and staying inside. Either course made sense.

But he had told Gabriella he'd protect her, and if he went outside, someone else could come in.

Which made the decision for him.

He straightened the covers, then stood by the bed, listening to the sound of running water in the bathroom and then the toilet flushing. He'd been alone for a long time, and it was strange to have someone else in the house.

Finally, Gabriella settled down, and he pictured her lying on the couch. Probably she hadn't taken her clothes off. He walked to the bedroom door and slipped out without looking in the direction of the couch. After making a quick trip to the bathroom, he returned to his room, laid down on his bed and tried to get comfortable, although he suspected that he wouldn't get much sleep.

His mind was still processing everything that had happened since he'd thrown Gabriella to the ground.

He'd thought that maybe one of the wiseguys from New Jersey had found him. And he still didn't know if he was in the clear. What if he had brought trouble to Gabriella just by choosing this plantation as a hideout?

And why had he come here, exactly?

He'd had the whole United States to choose from. Hell, the whole world. But when he left New Jersey, he headed southwest—and ended up in Lafayette. It had felt right to be here. Like the feeling when he decided to go after Rudy Maglioni.

He'd known the guy was dangerous, yet once he'd read about the mobster ordering the murder of a whole family because the father was in the witness protection program, Luke hadn't been able to walk away from his investigation.

Did being drawn to the right story mean he had some of the same psychic power as Gabriella? Maybe not the ability to see the future, but the ability to set himself on the right course, whatever that meant.

Or was he making stuff up, giving himself reasons to think he was like her in some way?

After stopping in Lafayette, he'd looked at the bulletin board in a local real estate office and seen that the Boudreaux plantation had furnished cottages for rent. There were other places in town he could have selected. Some of them were cheaper, but he hadn't looked at the others. Because, again, as soon as he'd read the listing, this was the one that seemed right. More than right. He'd felt as if he was on the brink of a discovery that had nothing to do with hiding out.

After weeks in the plantation rental house, he'd thought that he'd made up the notion about finding his destiny here—

until tonight, when he'd touched Gabriella. And his world had turned upside down.

Another line of thinking reemerged. If he'd brought trouble to the plantation, he'd have to leave, although the thought of clearing out made his chest tighten. He couldn't do it. Not until he and Gabriella had figured out why they'd gotten into each other's minds when they'd touched.

GABRIELLA HADN'T EXPECTED to sleep. But the emotional upheaval of the day finally exhausted her. When she woke just before dawn, she lay on the couch staring at the gray light outside the window and thinking about why she was here instead of at the main house. If she stayed on the couch, Luke would come out of the bedroom, and she'd have to confront him. That would be a hell of a morning after, especially because they hadn't done anything more than kiss.

They'd both wanted to go further. She couldn't lie about that. In some mysterious way, they'd exchanged memories. Underlying that was the strongest sexual pull she'd ever felt, coupled with a headache that was worse than anything she could remember.

Usually, she didn't even like being touched. When she'd made love with guys, she'd gotten drunk first to blunt the edge of her own reluctance. This morning when she thought about the sexual part with Luke, her body reacted. Which was reason enough to get out of here before the man in the bedroom woke up.

She hardly knew him. And she certainly didn't like being at the mercy of sexual feelings she couldn't explain.

Really, she should go back to New Orleans. Her mother's refusal to have a proper funeral had given her that option, but there was something she had to do before she left.

Mom had fallen down the stairs. There had to be a reason

why she'd been up there, and Gabriella wanted to know what it was.

And what about Luke Buckley? Did he represent something important to her, something she was trying to ignore?

Because she was afraid to explore it?

She clenched her teeth. She'd always longed for intimacy with someone. Now, here it was for the taking, and she was ready to walk away. Because she was a coward?

No, because she'd set herself on a life course, and she couldn't imagine simply abandoning her plans on a whim.

That was probably the wrong word, but she wasn't going to quibble about it now.

Quietly she picked up her shoes and tiptoed toward the door. On the porch, she stood in the chilly morning air, staring at the space between Cypress and the main house.

In the soft morning light, it looked just as it always did these days—in need of TLC. But she could imagine how it would look if she had the money to restore it's former grandeur.

For a moment, she let a little fantasy run through her mind. She could tell Emile to go to hell. She could take a loan on the house, come back here and fix the place up, then start a restaurant that would be the showplace of Lafayette. She was working as a pastry chef now, but she had the skills to do the rest of it. And the vision. It would be fun to go around to auctions and flea markets buying furnishings. Fun to make the gardens here look beautiful again. And fun to grow her own herbs and vegetables for the restaurant.

But she knew how much work the whole project would take. Really it would be better to have a partner who could handle the business end of it. And who would that be—because she didn't have any friends good enough to trust as a partner.

The image of Luke Buckley leaped into her mind. She

saw again his dark hair, a little too long. His strong jaw. His intense dark eyes.

She made a dismissive sound. Luke Buckley? She had to be kidding. She barely knew the man. And a few minutes ago she'd been talking herself into leaving the plantation before he woke up.

But she did know he had integrity. The mob had tried to intimidate him into dropping his book project, and he'd gone into hiding so he could finish writing before they killed him.

And once it was published, he was thinking they couldn't touch him because if they did, the whole world would know who had done it.

Which brought her back to the restaurant fantasy. He was a gambler, the perfect…

"Stop," she ordered herself. You are not going into business or anywhere else with Luke Buckley.

Quickly, she slipped on her shoes, then hurried across the lawn to the plantation house. Her keys were still in her pocket, and she paused to unlock the door, reassured to find that it was still secured. She locked it again behind her, then walked around turning off the lights that had been on when the power had gone off. Finally, she went back to the front hall and started up the stairs.

GEORGE CAMDEN WATCHED from the shadows of the trees as Gabriella Boudreaux crossed the scraggly lawn, then climbed the stairs and walked into the plantation house.

He'd gotten a little sleep in his car, then come back to check the cottage. Gabriella had been in the cottage. Now she was alone and unprotected. Nice of her to give him an opportunity to get her alone.

Had she ended up sleeping with the Buckley guy? Or did they have a falling out? That was more likely because she was in a tearing hurry to get away from his place.

The front door of the plantation house had been locked, but George had already figured out another way to get in. The house, like most of the ones in this low-lying area, had a raised basement. It had been a simple matter to remove the glass from one of the windows and put it back in place so it looked secure.

Waiting for a few minutes to make sure Gabriella wasn't coming out again, he circled the building, then ducked under the overhang at the edge of the basement area. The window was just as he'd left it. Careful not to make any noise, he lifted it out and set it along the wall. He'd laid a small outdoor end table on its side near the window, like somebody had thrown it there and forgotten it.

After righting the table, he placed it under the window and climbed up, then inside. Again he'd positioned a convenient piece of furniture—an old chest—where he could use it to climb down.

Inside, he stood listening for a few minutes. As far as he could tell, Gabriella hadn't heard him. He wasn't sure where she had gone, but he knew this was going to come out differently than with the mother.

LUKE HEARD GABRIELLA GET UP. He heard her tiptoe across the living room, heard the front door open.

She was sneaking out, and in a way he couldn't blame her, but he wasn't going to let her disappear so easily.

When he ran to the window of the cottage and looked out, he saw her crossing the lawn to the plantation house. To get her stuff and leave?

He was about to go back for his shoes when movement in the stand of trees to the side of the house made him freeze. A man emerged, checked to see that he was alone and looked toward the house. When he started to look back toward Cypress Cottage, Luke ducked to the side of the window.

Peering out again, he saw the intruder start for the house—not for the front. Instead, he circled around and disappeared from sight under the overhang of the raised basement.

Not good.

Luke had thought someone might be out here last night. It looked as if he had been right.

Was it a mobster? More likely someone interested in Gabriella because he'd gone after her and not come to the cottage. But it was clear that the guy was up to no good.

Otherwise he would have gone up and rung the doorbell.

AT THE TOP OF THE STAIRS, Gabriella paused. Nobody much had been up here in years, and the smell of dust was heavy in the air.

If she wanted to turn this place into a restaurant, the first thing she'd have to do was give the house a thorough cleaning.

"Forget the restaurant fantasy for now," she muttered as she looked one way down the hall and then the other. Finally, she couldn't resist peeking into her old bedroom.

It was the way she'd left it when she'd gone away to chef school. The curtains were drawn, making the light dim, but she could still see posters of kittens and puppies on the walls. How sappy!

But as a teenager, she'd related better to animals than she had to people.

In the hall again, she paused for a moment, unsure which way Mom had gone on her last trip up here. Too bad there wasn't enough dust on the floor to leave a trail of footprints.

Probably her best bet was Mom's old room. She stepped inside, looking around at the faded spread, the limp curtains, the antique furniture that was still in excellent shape.

Her gaze went to the dresser. People kept all kinds of intimate stuff in dresser drawers, but then when they died, someone else would poke through their possessions.

Like she was planning to do now.

After a moment's hesitation, she began searching the drawers. They held only a few articles of clothing and costume jewelry that her mother obviously hadn't been wearing lately.

Some dresses hung in the closet. All the clothes could go to one of the charities in town when Gabriella had the time to sort through them.

More interesting to her was the top shelf of the closet, which held several of the sturdy, rectangular boxes that department stores used to give away before they went to the cheap, fold up kind.

What was up there? Maybe what Gabriella was looking for.

She dragged the boxes down and took off the top of one, seeing a stack of papers. The next one held family photographs.

Not so secret. But maybe the secrets were mixed in with the normal stuff.

She was taking out a picture of Mom and Dad as newlyweds when the strong smell of cigarette smoke on clothing made her turn.

A man stepped into the doorway, his gaze fixed on her. He was tall, with dark hair, gray eyes and a predatory expression that sent a chill up her spine. Except for the look on his face, he was rather ordinary. A guy who could blend into a crowd.

Had she seen him before? Maybe, but there would have been no reason to remember him.

Her heart lurched inside her chest. "Who…who are you?" she asked stupidly.

Instead of answering the question, he said, "Come on. We're getting out of here."

"What do you want?"

"Shut up and do what I tell you."

Arguing was pointless. She thought about screaming for Luke's help. But he was too far away to hear. Could she get around the guy? Probably not. What about locking herself in the bathroom? Could she make it there before he grabbed her?

Her heart was pounding as she contemplated her options.

The man narrowed his eyes, pulling a gun from the waistband of his slacks. As he pointed it at her, he pulled a pair of handcuffs from another pocket.

"You're going to put them on."

She stared from the cuffs to the gun and back again, struggling to control her terror and thinking she should never have left Cypress Cottage on her own. Luke had been worried that someone was on the property. Apparently he'd been right, and she'd been too wound up in her own concerns to credit the warning. Well, that and the need to put some distance between them.

The man walked across the room, still holding the weapon pointed at her, then tossed the handcuffs onto the bed near her. "If you don't want to get shot, put them on."

All sorts of horrible thoughts raced through her mind. She remembered what she'd learned in self-defense classes. If someone took you out of your environment and had control over you, you were probably going to end up dead.

Mom had already ended up that way, and suddenly she thought—had this guy pushed her mother down the steps? And would he shoot now?

If the man used the gun, would Luke hear? Or was he still sleeping?

One thing she knew for sure—she wasn't putting on the

handcuffs. Not willingly. He'd have to knock her down first, maybe knock her out.

When the cuffs landed near the boxes, she pretended to follow his directions, seeing him relax a little. But instead of clicking them onto her wrists, she threw them at him as hard as she could, already ducking as she scrambled to get out of the line of fire. A shot whizzed over her head, and she knew that he hadn't been bluffing.

Now what? The bed was between them, and she heard him cursing as his footsteps came toward her.

There was nowhere to go. The window was behind her, but it was locked. And if she made a dash for it, he'd shoot her in the back. But maybe she *could* get into the bathroom and climb out the window onto the portico roof before he battered down the door.

"Bitch," the intruder snarled as he came around the bed.

This time she picked up the dusty throw rug and threw it at him.

He started coughing and slapping at the covering, apparently having trouble dislodging it with the gun in his hand—and also having trouble breathing through the dust.

Good.

But how long would the rug stop him?

Her only way out was across the bed, and she leaped onto it, listening intently for sounds behind her.

She knew he had finally gotten the rug off because his cursing was less muffled. She was almost to the edge of the mattress when he clamped his fingers around her ankle, preventing her from fleeing.

"You're going to be sorry about this," he growled as he pulled her across the bed.

She started kicking at him with her free leg, desperately trying to inflict damage while she struggled to get away.

When he whacked her shin with the side of the gun, she gritted her teeth and kept kicking.

The sound of pounding feet in the hall made them both look up.

Her back was to the door, but what the man saw made him turn her ankle loose and dodge back, aiming the gun at whoever was in the doorway.

# *Chapter Five*

Gabriella twisted around, goggling as she saw Luke leap into the room.

"He's got a gun," she shouted.

The gun went off, and she felt a bullet fly over her head.

"Luke," she screamed.

"Get down."

Ducking low, he charged at the man, who got off another shot, but Gabriella managed to kick his hand, making the shot go wild.

The intruder howled in frustration as Luke flung himself onto the bed.

The two men rolled back and forth across the spread, dropping to the floor, where they kept fighting, struggling for the weapon.

It discharged again, and one of them made a noise. Had Luke been hit?

He smashed at the guy's hand, banging the gun against the floor. It slipped from the man's grasp, and she darted forward, kicking it out of the way, then darted back. She couldn't shoot the guy and be sure she'd miss Luke.

Looking frantically around for a less lethal weapon, she picked up the lamp beside the bed, preparing to bash the intruder over the head. But again she hesitated. The men were moving too fast for her to be accurate.

The intruder must have reached the level of desperation. With a mighty heave, he threw Luke off of himself, scrambled up and charged out of the room.

She heard him taking the stairs two at a time. Moments later the front door slapped open.

When she ran to the window, she saw him tearing across the lawn.

"Where's he going?" Luke asked from the floor.

"Into the woods. It looks like he's cutting his losses."

"Good. But we can't take that for granted. I mean," he clarified in a gritty voice, "we have to get out of here."

He was right. The guy could come back. Turning toward Luke, she knelt beside him and saw a red stain on his shirt sleeve.

When she gasped, he looked down at the blood spreading across the fabric and blinked.

"Just a flesh wound," he said.

"How do you know?"

Cautiously, he moved the arm and winced. "Logical deduction. It would hurt like hell if it hit the bone, and it didn't hit an artery—or the blood would be coming out like a fountain."

"Thank goodness." She dragged in a breath and let it out. "How did you know the guy came in?"

"I heard you get up. Saw you leave. I was going to come over here when I saw him slip out of the shadows under the trees and head for the house."

"Thank goodness," she said again. "I'd better look at your arm."

He tensed when she reached for his hand. She was so focused on the wound that she'd forgotten about why she'd wanted to get away from him. Thinking that she might have to rip his sleeve to see the injury, she caught his wrist.

But the moment her fingers brushed his flesh, she forgot

what she'd been about to do. Forgot everything but the two of them.

It was like the first time they'd touched, only more intense, the experience jolted up by her almost getting kidnapped and by Luke's appearance just in the nick of time. Or perhaps it was because they were touching for the second time.

All she knew was that one moment she was thinking clearly. In the next, sensations grabbed her. Sensations and the thoughts swirling in his consciousness.

She was in his mind, watching him listen to her leaving Cypress. He went to the window of the cottage—looking at her—his stomach knotting as he realized she intended to slip away while he was still sleeping.

Then he saw the man sneaking around the house and knew she was in trouble.

Forcing himself to wait until the guy had disappeared, he followed with his heart pounding and found the window that had been removed.

She saw all that. Felt his concern for her as he entered the house, listening for sounds, trying to figure out where she was and where the intruder was without giving himself away.

At the same time, she knew he was pulling her own recent memories from her mind. Coming up here to search for clues to what her mother had been doing. Taking down the boxes. Her shock and fear when she saw the guy in the doorway. Saw the gun and the handcuffs.

The terror of a few minutes ago when she'd been fighting for her life blended with her present emotions as Luke gathered her closer, tenderly and at the same time with an edge of passion.

Heat leaped between them as he lowered his mouth to hers, moving his lips in an act of seduction that was sweet and hot all at the same time.

*Open for me.*

*Oh, yes.*

He hadn't spoken aloud, but she heard the words inside her head.

She did as he asked, loving the way his tongue played with the sensitive tissue of her inner lips, then went farther, tracing the edges of her teeth, then finding her tongue.

The headache was back, but she ignored it.

Her pulse had been pounding with fear. Now it pounded with the blood suddenly rushing hotly through her veins.

She felt more than her own desire. She felt his also. And under the passion, the blinding dread he'd felt when he'd known she was in danger.

She thought again that she hardly knew him. But it was a notion she'd clung to because she was coping with the unknown. They were important to each other in ways she couldn't name. But she didn't have to put a label on it to know it was true.

That knowledge led to a deeper truth. She wanted him in every possible way. Mind. Body. Heart.

And it was the same for him. She read that in the way his mouth moved urgently over hers. More than that, she saw his intentions. He was going to lie back on the rug, taking her with him until her body was sprawled on top of his. She liked the idea. Felt the same overwhelming urge to finish what they had started the night before.

But when he moved his hand to cup her breast, she felt the pain in his arm lace through him. Pain he'd apparently forgotten about as soon as she'd touched him.

Drawing back, she made a small sound of shock at her reckless disregard for him.

"What are we doing? You're hurt."

"Apparently it slipped my mind," he answered ruefully, looking as dazed as she felt.

While they both struggled to drag in air, she drew back, deliberately breaking the physical contact as she stared at him, trying to collect her scattered wits. "We have to…to fix your arm. Then we have to get out of here."

"Yeah. But you've got it in reverse order. You brought an overnight bag?"

"It's still in my car."

"I have to get a few things from the cottage."

"Now who's the one with his priorities screwed up?"

"Not me. I need my laptop. And my research materials. I'm not going anywhere without them."

"Yes, right." She remembered, then, how important the book was to him. Important enough to risk his life.

He was already pushing himself up. She would have helped him, but after the way heat had flared between them, she was afraid to touch him. If she did, they'd both forget what they were supposed to be doing.

He stood on legs that weren't entirely steady, bracing his good arm against the wall as he started toward the door.

"I'll be right there," she murmured.

"I'm not letting you out of my sight again."

"We should take the gun. And…" She gestured toward the papers she'd thrown at the intruder. "And this stuff. I think this may be what my mom went upstairs to get."

"Why?"

"There's nothing else important up here."

He looked torn. Finally he answered with a tight nod and leaned against the wall with his eyes closed, and she felt guilt about making him wait.

"You should sit down."

"If I do, I may not get back up."

"You're in shock."

"Maybe."

She wasn't going to waste time arguing with him. Instead,

she quickly put the papers back in the box. There were also plastic bags in the closet, and she slipped the box into one to make carrying easier.

"Okay."

She saw him collecting his strength before the trip to the first floor.

When they reached the step, she dragged in a quick breath.

"What?"

"My mom…fell here. Unless, of course, he pushed her."

"Yeah. It could have been him. He'd already fixed himself up a way to get inside."

"I guess he was the stalker she called about." She gave Luke a considering look as she switched to practical matters. "You're not exactly steady on your feet. Maybe I should go first."

She moved around him, walking down a few steps and waiting for him to follow.

He came cautiously after her. Once he did miss his footing, but his good hand was clutching the banister, and he kept from tumbling into her.

"I'll drive you to Cypress."

He snorted. "I'm not an invalid."

"Oh, right. Just shot in the arm. The bullet could still be in there."

"I don't think so."

She went into the kitchen and retrieved the spare set of car keys that she kept at Mom's. With the gun in one hand and the keys in the other, she walked to the front door and looked out. What if the attacker had come back and was waiting for them to emerge? Did he know that Luke was shot and that he only had to contend with the woman he'd come to abduct?

Why had he tried to take her? It had to be something specific to *her*. But what?

She saw no sign of the man, but she hadn't seen him before he'd stepped into the bedroom, and he had obviously been hanging around. Yesterday and today.

Dragging in a breath, she searched the air for the smell of cigarette smoke on clothing, but she didn't detect any.

Still, she kept alert as she hurried down the steps and unlocked the car, then motioned for Luke to follow. Again, he walked painfully and slowly as he descended the outside steps, and she had to bite back the need to help him.

As he reached the car, she looked back at the front door. Should she lock the house? Or was that a lost cause? Obviously the guy had figured out how to get in without the key.

When she looked back at Luke, he was sitting in the front seat inspecting the grounds the way she had.

"Lock the front door," he muttered.

"Are you reading my mind?"

"No. Just being logical. You don't want someone else coming in."

"What about the window?"

He cursed. "Yeah. Forgot about that. I think we need to make it look like it's intact."

"We need to see how badly you're hurt."

"Like I said, we have to prioritize. Do the damn window first. Then we can leave as soon as we've got my stuff."

Staying out in the open made her nervous, but she drove around the side of the house and found the missing window. The whole thing had been removed and set against the wall. At least it wasn't broken. Leaving the engine running, she climbed out of the car and lifted the frame and window into place. It fit into the molding, and when she stepped back, it wasn't obvious that it had been removed and replaced.

"We should call the police," she said when she returned to the car.

"In my experience, it's better to leave the cops out of the equation unless you've got a body on your hands."

She winced. "Why?"

"What are you planning to tell them? That someone broke in?"

"Yes. At least they can keep an eye on the property."

"Are you going to tell them someone tried to kidnap you?"

She thought about that.

"If you do, they'll have a lot of questions. And we're going to have to report a gunshot wound—which I don't want to do."

When she started to speak, he plowed ahead.

"Because it's safer just to get the hell out of here."

She thought about his reasoning. "Okay."

"Then you'd better tell your boss you're not coming in."

"Damn! I wasn't even thinking about that."

"Which?"

"My job."

"You can say you need to take care of some stuff down here."

"He'll tell me not to bother showing up."

"He's that much of a bastard?"

"Afraid so."

She studied Luke's pale face and decided not to tire him out with any more conversation about their strategy or the trials of working with Emile Gautreaux. Instead, she backed up and looped down the drive, taking the cutoff to the cottages.

The door to Cypress wasn't locked, and she hesitated. "He could be in there."

Luke pressed past her. "Give me the gun."

She wanted to protest, but she handed over the weapon and watched while he stepped into the cottage. Unwilling to wait outside, she followed him in, where he checked the rooms.

"Clear, as they say on the cop shows." He went to his desk and sat down heavily, then began opening drawers and pulling out papers, stuffing them into a briefcase.

"Can I help?" she asked.

"I have a duplicate set. One for me and one for my editor."

"It's all on paper?"

"No. It's mostly the same as my computer files." He turned and looked at her. "If anything happens to me, make sure they get to Parker and Sons in New York."

"Nothing's going to happen to you."

"Yeah. Right." He looked toward the bedroom. "I keep a bag packed. It's tan. In the bottom of the closet. Can you bring that, too?"

"Yes."

When she returned, he was sitting with his eyes closed and the gun in his lap. Hearing her, he snapped to attention, but she saw his skin was clammy and beads of perspiration had broken out on his forehead.

She gave him a critical look. "Your arm…"

"When we get out of here."

"You're putting your health in danger."

"It's going to be in more danger if that guy comes back to shoot us."

"You think he will?"

"I don't know how desperate he is."

"Desperate—that's an interesting way to put it."

He jammed a baseball cap on his head so that the bill partly hid his face. "There's a jacket in the closet. I'd better put it on to hide the bloodstain."

"That will hurt."

"Yeah. But nobody's going to forget a guy with a bloody shirt."

She brought a light jacket and helped him into it without touching him through the fabric. She could tell that moving his arm hurt like the devil and he was sweating badly by the time they finished.

"Give me one of the bags, and let's get out of here."

She understood he was right about leaving, but she wasn't going to let him do any work.

"No. You, uh, get in your car and cover me."

"My car? Why?"

She scrambled for a good reason. "Just a feeling I have—that we should take it."

When he got up, his teeth were clenched, but he said nothing as he opened the door and stood surveying the area. Then he started painfully down the steps. He made it to the car and sat watching the surrounding area while she put the first load in the trunk.

His face looked gray. How long could you let his wound go without treating it? She glanced at his laptop. Probably she could find out on the web. But that would only waste more time.

Grimly she carried his papers and the tan bag out of the cottage and put them in the trunk, along with her own overnight bag and the desserts she'd brought.

When she climbed in, Luke breathed out a small sigh.

"Where are we going exactly?" she asked.

"There's a motel about twenty miles from here. The Lazy Bayou. It's not…plush, but I wasn't thinking I'd be taking anyone with me."

"Why were you looking for a motel?"

"In case I had to get out of here in a hurry. Come on. You can call your boss when we get there."

"I've put you in danger. Gotten you shot," she whispered.

"I was having the same thought—about the danger part.

When I didn't know your attacker wasn't one of the New Jersey mobsters."

"You don't think he's one of them now, right?"

"Do you?"

"No."

"Let's get out of here."

Lips set in a grim line, she started toward the access road that led to the highway when a flash of sunlight made her stop abruptly, pitching Luke forward before he settled back in his seat.

He groaned.

"Sorry."

"What was that?"

"I spotted a car down on the driveway."

Luke peered down the access road. "Where?"

"You can't see it. I wouldn't have known it was there except that the sun just glared off his windshield. It must be him—waiting for us."

# *Chapter Six*

Gabriella watched Luke's expression turn angry. "Tricky bastard! Is there some other way out of here?"

"There's a back way through the swamp, but it could be under water for all I know."

"We have to chance it."

As she backed up, they saw the other car coming toward them. He must have seen her change direction and figured he could cut them off.

"Lucky I've got four-wheel drive."

She headed past the house, watching the rearview mirror as much as the barely visible road in front of her.

Luke twisted around and winced. "I'll keep track of him."

"His name is George," she said.

"What?"

"George."

"How do you know?"

"I just do. I mean, it leaped into my mind," she said as she focused on the rutted dirt road that led back into the plantation grounds. Long ago she'd played in what she called "the wilderness," but she hadn't been through here in years, and she had no idea if the road was even passable.

Still, she kept going because she had no other choice. The lane wound under the trees, where the thick foliage instantly darkened their surroundings. She wanted to turn on the lights, but the guy would see them in the gloom, so she kept driving until she suddenly had to slam on the brakes.

"What?" Luke asked.

"A tree across the road."

"Can you go around?"

"I don't know."

"Try!" She heard Luke's frustration. Probably he wished he were driving, but that was out of the question.

As soon as she turned off the road into a flat area, she could feel mud sucking at the tires but she kept moving, bouncing over ruts and splashing through puddles and avoiding other fallen logs that partially blocked the way. As two deer sprinted in front of them, she braked hard, making the car rock.

When she tried to start up again, the wheels spun, and panic made her grip the wheel.

Luke turned toward her. "Don't tense up."

"I'm trying not to."

"Back up and ease forward."

When she tried to follow his suggestion, nothing happened. A panicked glance in the rearview mirror told her that the other car was weaving through the trees, coming at them.

"He's going to get us," she gasped.

"No. I'm going to push."

Her breath caught in her throat. "You can't."

"The hell I can't."

Luke clambered out and got in back of the car. "When I call 'now,' press on the accelerator."

She wanted to scream at him that he was crazy, but she knew they had to escape. Looking out the side mirror, she saw Luke had turned sideways, positioning his good shoulder against the back of the car.

When he shouted, she gunned the engine. At first she was

sure they were stuck for all eternity. Gritting her teeth, she gave the car gas slowly, forcing herself not to stab down on the accelerator. Finally, after centuries, the car lurched forward, and Luke ran around to the passenger side, jumping in and slamming the door behind him.

George, if that was his real name, was almost on them. As she tried to put distance between the two cars, Luke leaned out the door, the gun in his hand.

He fired behind them, and the other vehicle stopped abruptly.

"Did you hit him?" she panted as she wove her way back onto the road.

"I wasn't trying to hit him. I was just trying to make him think it was a bad idea to follow us." He cursed.

"What?"

"I forgot the damn gun I keep in the nightstand."

"Don't worry about it now."

"Stupid!"

"You were thinking of other stuff."

She could hear the engine of the other car roaring as the guy behind them tried to get out of the same mud where she'd been mired.

For the moment, he was stuck. But they still weren't out of the woods. The narrow track was now slick with scummy water, but at least there was some gravel helping to make the surface less slippery.

Praying that they didn't wind up in a lake, she kept going, stopping once and backing up so she could go down the side of the road where the water didn't look too deep.

Beside her Luke was breathing hard. And when she glanced at him, his face was pale as death.

"Luke?"

He gritted his teeth, and she couldn't stop herself from covering his hand with hers. Instantly, pain leaped through her, pain so bad that she almost lost control of the vehicle and crashed into a tree.

Somehow she managed to stay on the road because that was her job.

"Oh, my," she whispered.

"I'll be okay."

"You..."

"Wrenched my arm. I'll be okay."

When she heard the pain in his voice and felt it echoing through her, she ached to stop and take him in her arms. Or tear off his jacket and shirt and have a look at the wound.

"It won't do you much good out here," he said, apparently picking up on her thoughts.

"I threw a first-aid kit into the car."

"Later. Keep going," he ordered. "We don't know when he'll get free."

She clamped her hands on the wheel, forcing her attention back to the driving, praying that they would get to the motel soon.

He glanced behind him.

"Can you see him?"

"He's still stuck. Just keep going. Not too fast."

She agreed, but it was difficult to keep from pressing down heavily on the gas pedal.

The track was barely passable, and it got worse the farther they drove. She was thinking that they were going to bog down again when she saw the blessed blacktop of the highway ahead. No stretch of road had ever looked more welcome.

Just before pulling onto the highway, she opened the door and inspected the side of the vehicle. It looked like an elephant after a mud bath.

"Which way?" she asked Luke, who was leaning heavily against the headrest.

His eyes blinked open.

"Where are we in relationship to the plantation's main entrance?"

"About a mile east."

"Turn left. Keep going until you see a commercial area."

After giving her directions to the Lazy Bayou, he leaned back and closed his eyes again, and she thought he was probably at the end of his resources. His skin was white, and sweat wet his brow. She wanted to reach out and cup his forehead to find out if he had a fever. But touching him was a bad idea.

*Yeah.*

The agreement echoed in her mind.

"You were thinking that, too?"

"Uh-huh."

His voice sounded thin. He didn't speak again, and when she glanced at him, she knew that he had drifted off to sleep.

While she headed for the motel he'd mentioned, she reached for her cell phone. As she had the day before, she took a chance on talking while driving.

Tommy, one of the assistant chefs, picked up on the second ring.

"Chez Emile's."

"It's Gabriella."

"Gabriella, where are you?"

"Long story. Is Emile there?"

"Yeah. And he's annoyed with you. He was expecting you back this morning. There's a big list of desserts you're supposed to do."

"I assume other people are filling in for me."

"Yeah."

"Let me talk to him," she said, wondering exactly what she was going to say.

As soon as Emile picked up the phone, he took control of the conversation.

"Gabriella, where the hell are you?"

"Emile, my mother died. There are some things I need to take care of down here," she answered, pretending that was the reason for her absence.

"I'm sorry about your mother," he said in a grudging voice. "But you should have called last night."

"I was caught up in…the arrangement," she answered. It wasn't exactly a lie, depending on your definition. "It will be a few days before I can get back to town," she added.

"We have a lot to do here. Remember, that congressional delegation is coming for dinner."

"Oh, right. Sorry."

The dinner was a big deal for Emile, but she'd forgotten all about it.

"I have Janie covering for you. And I took on a new guy to fill in. He's a graduate of L'Academie de Cuisine in D.C."

"That's good," she answered, wondering if it was—from her point of view.

"Janie is doing a wonderful job. We may not need you."

"I…"

"I'm sorry, I have to keep up the restaurant's standards."

She couldn't stop herself from challenging him. "What if I were sick? Would you just let me go?"

"I'm sorry, Gabriella. We can talk when you're back in town and feeling more yourself," he said before clicking off, leaving her listening to dead air.

Numbly, she put away the phone. She'd expected Emile to be angry that she wasn't giving him top priority, but not to, in effect, fire her. What a self-centered jerk. He owed her back pay, which she was damn well going to collect when she got the chance.

Which was when, exactly? Certainly not until they'd dealt with the man chasing her.

When she slowed at the entrance to the Lazy Bayou Motel, Luke jerked awake, looking wildly around.

"What?"

"The motel."

"Don't stop yet."

"Why not?"

"Because we're hiding out, and I don't want the clerk to see a woman in the car. George, if that's his name, is looking for you. I want you to lie down in the back. I'll drive in and get the room."

"You can't drive in your condition."

"We're not going far."

She gave him a critical inspection. He still looked like hell. But she understood the wisdom of his plan. After continuing past the motel, she pulled into the parking lot of a fast food restaurant, where she got into the backseat while Luke eased behind the wheel. She wanted to ask if he was going to pass out, but she kept her mouth shut as she scrunched down and tried to get comfortable on the floor mat.

She heard Luke cursing under his breath as he turned the car around. His driving was jerky, and she prayed that he could make it as far as the motel. The car turned in and lurched to a stop, a few feet from the front wall of the office, but she didn't comment.

"Stay here," he ordered, then got out and walked toward the building. "And stay down."

She did as he asked, hoping he didn't pass out before getting them a room.

One room, of course. Which would mean there was no way to avoid touching him. She thought of the implications and shivered with a mixture of anticipation and dread.

LUKE STEADIED HIMSELF against the car door as he looked around. They were in a rural location, backing up to a wooded area and probably a bayou.

He dragged in several breaths and let them out, trying to compose himself as much as possible.

The bullet had knocked the stuffing out of him, but he had to think it wasn't actually life threatening, or he'd already be out cold.

He glanced into the car and saw that Gabriella had followed directions. She was one hell of a woman. Too bad he hadn't met her under calmer circumstances. There was something between them that the two of them had to explore, but it would have to wait.

Simply walking across the gravel parking lot to the office door used up most of his energy. If he were honest, he would admit that he was in no shape to be on his feet.

He gritted his teeth. He wasn't going to admit to Gabriella that it hurt like hell. But he didn't have to. She'd picked it up from his mind.

He paused to adjust his baseball cap so that it partially covered his features, then took a breath and opened the door.

A bell rang, but nobody was in the office.

Damn. Just what he needed. A delay.

"Anybody home?" he called out as he leaned against the counter to stay upright.

A young man with short blond hair and a long face came running from a room in back of the counter. Not the same guy Luke had talked to before, which was probably a good thing. One meeting would make him less memorable.

"Sorry about that," the clerk said. "I was in the can."

"No problem," Luke answered in a mild tone when he wanted to snap at the guy. Which was a good indication that he was in bad shape because he didn't lose his cool easily.

"What can I do for you?"

Luke was tempted to answer sarcastically that he wanted to order an alligator dinner. Instead, he said, "I'm doing some wildlife photography in the area, and I need a room for a couple of nights."

The clerk peered at him, and he resisted the impulse to pull the cap farther down over his face. "You okay, buddy?"

He forced a laugh, wishing he'd thought about his story before he'd opened his mouth. "Well, that's not the only reason I'm in town. My friend's getting married. We've been doin' a little celebrating."

The clerk made a disparaging sound. "Hope he's still celebrating this time next year."

"You and me both. That woman has him running in circles already."

Luke filled out the registration form, giving a fake license plate number.

"You got a quiet room around the back where I can sleep off this hangover?" he asked.

"Number fifteen."

"Thanks."

He thought about the guy looking for them. Would he check at every motel in a fifty-mile radius? Farther? Would he think they'd tried to get as far away as possible before stopping? Luke cast around for some way he could ensure that the clerk wouldn't talk about him if asked.

When he shifted his weight from one foot to the other, the man behind the counter gave him an inquiring look.

He cleared his throat, deciding he might as well spin another story. "My buddy and I got into some trouble last night. Some guys might come looking for me." He pulled out his wallet and extracted fifty dollars. "If someone comes asking questions, I'd appreciate a call in my room."

The clerk accepted the money. "Sure."

Would he do it? Would he even be here if the man looking for them showed up?

He had no way of answering the questions and no energy to reinforce the request. He'd done all he could—short of putting a hundred miles between them and the guy Gabriella called George. And that wasn't going to happen.

He made it out of the office, sweating heavily as he wove his way back to the car.

From the floor of the backseat, Gabriella gave him a long look as he climbed back behind the wheel. "Did he ask you if you wanted a hospital bed?"

Luke glanced back at the office window. "He thinks I've got a hangover from a hard night of partying."

"I guess that's as good an excuse as any for looking like hell."

"The room's in back where nobody could see the car from the road. Number fifteen."

He drove around the end of the building, where there was another row of rooms similar to the ones in front.

The parking lot bordered on the wooded area they'd seen from the road.

His energy level falling rapidly, Luke climbed out and headed for the motel room door. But when he got there, he wasn't quite able to insert the key in the lock.

"Let me," Gabriella said gently.

He held out the thick plastic disk with a fifteen printed on it. She took it without allowing their fingers to touch and opened the door, stepping aside so he could enter.

The room was shabby but clean, with a queen-size bed, dresser, older model TV, and table and chairs by the window. He wanted to flop right onto the bed; instead, he stood swaying in the center of the worn carpet.

"Maybe it's better not to get blood on the spread."

She made an anxious sound as she rushed over and pulled

down the covers. He kicked off his shoes, collapsed gratefully onto the bed and lay with his eyes closed. The damn arm was throbbing like crazy, probably because he should have gotten horizontal hours ago. But when could he have done it?

"I need to look at your wound," she said.

"Need to sleep," he said, hearing his own slurred speech.

"After I look at the arm," she said, her voice making it clear that she wasn't going to leave him alone until he complied. And she was probably right. Maybe he should delegate the thinking to her for the time being.

He sat up. Teeth gritted, he tried to pull off his jacket. Gabriella helped him, keeping her hands on the sleeves.

There was more blood on the shirt than previously. Probably he'd opened up the hole when he'd pushed the car.

She made a little gasping sound.

"It's all right," he reassured her as he started to work the buttons, but he couldn't open them.

When he gave her an angry look, she came over and sat on the side of the bed. "I'll do it."

"I thought you didn't want to touch me."

"I'll try not to."

When she reached to slip open one of the buttons, her finger brushed against his chest, and they both went very still.

"Oh, my," she breathed. "I just caught a little…sample of what you're feeling now."

"I'll be okay."

"I hope," she murmured as she opened the next button. He kept his gaze down, but she couldn't stop the emotions zinging back and forth between them. She felt shaken by the attack and guilty because he'd come to her rescue and gotten hurt.

"It's okay," he murmured.

"It's my problem, not yours."

"No," he answered, the denial automatic.

*He was after me, not you.*

He had picked that up from her mind. Because they were touching. He tried to focus on her thoughts, but he couldn't even keep his own straight.

She was still struggling with the shirt, and he knew that if he had to sit here much longer, he would pass out.

*Just rip off the damn thing,* he shouted inside his mind.

"What?"

"Sorry." He made an attempt to keep his voice even. "Rip it off. It's ruined anyway."

GABRIELLA HAD GROWN UP in a household where every penny was carefully budgeted. Destroying clothing went against every value that she'd been taught since childhood. But she saw the logic of his suggestion. She also knew that pain was driving him past frustration.

"I'll help," he said through gritted teeth.

He held one side of the front with his good hand. She yanked at the other, and the remaining buttons popped off and flew in all directions.

Luke worked his good hand out of the sleeve, and she grasped the fabric, pulling it free. It was clear that the effort had exhausted him, and he fell back against the pillows, breathing hard.

Remembering the first-aid kit in the car, she said, "I'll be right back."

When she returned to the room, Luke's eyes flew open in alarm.

"Just me."

"Yeah. I'm..."

"Jumpy. We both are."

She sat down on the edge of the bed and took a small

pair of scissors from the kit, which she used to slit the other sleeve from cuff to shoulder. Gingerly, she pulled it away. The shirt was a mess, and she worked the pieces off that had stuck to his skin and dropped them in the trash can.

For a moment, her gaze was captured by the broad expanse of his naked chest. He said he spent a lot of time at his desk, but he must work out because he was in fantastic shape. But she wasn't supposed to be admiring his masculine physique. She was supposed to be finding out how badly he was hurt.

Leaning down, she inspected the wound, seeing that the bullet had plowed along the side of his upper arm, making a long red track in the skin, sort of like an arm bracelet. Only it was dug into the flesh and crusted with dried blood.

"I think you were damn lucky," she said as she inspected the site.

He looked at the damage. "I told you it wasn't serious. It just hurts like the devil because it tore up a lot of skin."

There was antiseptic in the kit. With a gauze pad, she slathered it on the wound, then used several pads and a length of gauze tied around his arm as a covering. She couldn't do it without touching him briefly. As she did, she sensed a welter of confused thoughts from him.

He was thinking about the mob. About the night before when they'd kissed. His terror when he'd realized the guy was following her into the house.

Then the thoughts stopped abruptly, and panic leaped in her chest.

When she looked into his face and saw the even rise and fall of his chest, she knew that he had lost the battle to stay awake.

He was lying at the edge of the bed, leaving room for her to slip onto the other side and lie down without touching him.

First she walked to the window and closed the blind,

thinking she should have done that earlier. Then, because it was now dark in the room, she turned on the bathroom light and cracked the door in case he woke later in a strange room and needed the bathroom.

Which wasn't such a bad idea, come to think of it.

She used the facilities, then washed her hands and face, feeling marginally better. She would have liked a shower, but then she wouldn't be able to hear him if he needed her. Instead, she stood at the sink and took off her shirt and bra, using a washcloth to refresh herself before drying off and putting on her shirt.

She was wrung out in ways she hadn't been able to imagine. The emotional toll of her mother's death would have been enough to deal with. But she was also trying to cope with the weird bond between herself and Luke—and the knowledge that a man was hunting them. No, hunting *her.* Whatever Luke thought about it, she knew that was true.

Barely able to stay vertical now, she kicked off her shoes and eased onto the bed, being careful to keep some distance between herself and Luke. Too bad this room didn't have two beds. But he couldn't have asked for that because he was supposed to be alone.

Simply lying down was a luxury. It felt wonderful to relax. At least as much as she could relax when she knew that George was still out there somewhere.

She glanced over at Luke, reassured by the rise and fall of his broad chest. She'd never felt comfortable with physical contact. But the desire to touch this man was overwhelming. Something happened when they touched. Something she couldn't explain, but it set off cravings inside her that were stronger than anything she'd felt before in her life.

How ironic. She'd avoided touch. Now she longed for it, and at the same time she knew that she couldn't simply take what she wanted. She'd wake Luke up and set off feelings they couldn't deal with now.

Abandoning irony, she switched to practicalities. They'd pulled the bedding down so she could tend his arm. Forcing herself to move, she dragged it back into place, covering his chest.

Again she switched gears as she realized the two of them were under the covers together.

In the warmth of the bed, her fingers flexed, but she kept her arm at her side. He was hurt. He needed to rest. To heal. And then…

She might try to deny it, but she knew what was going to happen. It had to.

Closing her eyes, she let herself drift. Just for a while. When she was feeling a little less fatigued, she could get up and move to the chair.

# Chapter Seven

George Camden had a rich selection of curses at his disposal, some of them picked up in prison by listening to experts. He used them all, including choice nouns and adjectives to describe the woman who had led him into the swamp where his car had gotten stuck in the mud.

By the time he'd finally gotten himself out, he'd figured there was no way to catch up with them. Instead of trying to drive through more of the muck, he'd turned around and exited the way he'd come in, then circled back around to the plantation.

Probably there was no point in going inside the big house again. It wouldn't give any clues to where they'd gone. But the cottage was another matter. The guy had been living there, and maybe he'd know some place where they could go to hide.

They'd locked the door, but this time George didn't bother with the niceties of removing a whole window. He simply broke a pane of glass around back where it wouldn't be easily spotted and reached inside to spring the lock.

Once inside the cottage, he started looking around. Buckley had left some clothing in the closet and a gun in the nightstand. George appropriated it. Then, with an angry snort, he yanked a shirt off a hanger and took it into the bathroom, where he scuffed off his filthy shoes, put them in the sink and used the shirt and running water to clean the mess. Then he tossed the muddy rag on the middle of the bathtub. That made him feel a little better.

The clean shoes gave him an idea. Because Gabriella and the guy weren't coming back, he figured he had some time. In the bathroom, he stripped off his dirty clothes and took a shower. Then he grabbed a pair of the guy's slacks and put them on. They were a little long, but that was okay.

Finally back on an even keel, he started looking around for anything else useful. The guy had cleared out the papers and computer that George had seen through the window on a previous visit. Under the edge of the chair he saw some of the papers Gabriella had gone upstairs to get. But they didn't tell him anything new.

Then he found another kind of clue. Blood on the arm of a chair. Buckley must have gotten hit when they'd been wrestling for the gun and it had gone off.

How bad?

Well, not bad enough to keep him from clearing stuff out. Or from pushing the car, for that matter. But he was bleeding. In pain. How far was he going to go in that kind of condition? Even with the woman driving.

George looked out the front window. Where would a bleeding guy go? Maybe he'd have to head straight to the hospital if the wound was bad enough.

Or maybe not if he thought he had to hide out. From the blood on the chair and what George remembered of the fight, it was a good bet Buckley was hit in the arm. Was the bullet still in him? If it was, he might be reluctant to explain what had happened. Still, the hospitals would be the first place to check. Then motels in the area. Then motels a little farther away. But which direction would they go?

He cursed again, hating the way the interfering renter had

whacked up his plans. But he'd get back on track. He had to because he knew the Badger was getting antsy.

"Speak of the devil," he muttered when his cell phone rang. He wanted to ignore it, but he figured he'd better answer.

"Do you have the daughter?" the Badger asked straight off the bat.

"She's hooked up with her mom's tenant."

"The Luke Buckley guy?"

"Yes."

"I did a background check on him. He doesn't have any."

"The name's made up," George conceded.

"You knew that and you didn't tell me?"

"It wasn't relevant."

"I'll be the judge of that," the Badger said with a dangerous edge in his voice. "You understand?"

"Yes."

"Call me as soon as you have the daughter."

George wanted to ask why she was so important, but he'd learned to keep his mouth shut and follow directions.

The line went dead, leaving him with a queasy feeling.

GABRIELLA GASPED. She must have gone to sleep, but now she was standing in a room she didn't recognize, staring at a man with a knife. His hardened features had solidified into a satisfied look.

"When I'm finished with you, there won't be a piece large enough to feed to the dogs."

She didn't answer. She could barely drag air into her lungs. And she knew at that terrible moment that she was dreaming, but it wasn't *her* dream. It was Luke's.

No, someone named Liam Bridges. That was his real name, she thought with the part of her mind that was still detached from him.

Was the man one of the mobsters after him? Or was this something else that had happened to him? What kind of dangerous life had he chosen for himself?

Or was it just a nightmare he'd conjured out of his pain and the knowledge that they were being hunted by a killer?

The part of her that was still Gabriella wanted to shout to him to wake up, but in the dream, she *was* him. Which meant she couldn't talk to him. Or could she. You talk to yourself inside your mind, don't you?

Her head spun as she tried to puzzle that out, and her heart pounded as she waited for the man with the knife to strike.

He leaped at Luke, who stood his ground, letting the guy come, then went into some kind of fighting mode that she didn't understand. Dodging just far enough to the side to avoid the knife, he stuck out a foot, tripping the attacker so that he went down, his own knife driving into his chest.

Luke looked at the man on the floor, then calmly reached out and picked up the phone. She knew he was calling the police.

Before he could speak, the scene changed. She was a young boy, running down the sidewalk, trying to get away from a bigger kid, Sunny Wilcox, who liked to wait behind a fence for the little guys and beat the crap out of them.

Only Liam Bridges had been ready for him. As he rounded a corner he reached into his pocket and brought out two of those rolls of pennies. He wrapped his little fists around the red tubes, and when Wilcox caught up with him and spun him around, he struck with one hand, then the other, pounding the bigger boy with the makeshift weapons until he went down on his knees.

Satisfied that the bully wasn't going to attack again, Liam took off. He had escaped from Wilcox, but another scene grabbed him. This time a younger boy was screaming, flailing in the water, and Liam jumped in, grabbed the drowning kid, then struggled to get them both to shore, only the other boy was hitting him, and they were both going down, choking.

Gasping for air, summoning every ounce of resolve she could muster, Gabriella wrenched herself awake, finding that Luke had moved next to her in his sleep, his naked arm pressed to hers, which was why she'd been pulled into his dream.

She rolled away from him, breathing hard, struggling for coherence.

"Luke, Luke," she cried out. "You're having a nightmare. Wake up."

She wanted to shake him, but she knew she couldn't touch him now.

"Liam," she tried. "Liam."

At the sound of the other name, his eyes blinked open, and he stared at her in the dim light. He was obviously trying to orient himself in time and space.

"Sunny Wilcox..." he said in a muzzy voice.

"He was in your nightmare."

He blinked. "Gabriella?"

"Yes."

"What..."

"You were having a nightmare," she repeated.

He flopped to his back and cursed under his breath. "Did I drag you with me?"

"I...I don't know if you dragged me. But...I was there."

"Sorry."

"It's okay."

"No." His eyes took on a faraway look, and she knew he was being drawn back to the frightening scenes.

"Was all that real? Or did you conjure it up?"

He huffed out a breath. "It was real. My sordid past."

"Not sordid. Protective. Brave. Effective."

He snorted, but she knew the dream was another shortcut to understanding this man.

While she was thinking of what to say, he muttered, "I don't usually have nightmares. Sorry."

"Not your fault. You've had a rough day."

She was acutely aware of the intimacy of the moment. She'd shared his dream. Now she was lying beside him in bed. She ached to touch him, to comfort him. To feel his emotions surge through her, but she knew it wouldn't be a good idea.

"Was the first guy from the mob?"

He laughed. "No. That was a few years ago. He was sent by another lowlife. A Newark drug dealer who didn't like what I was writing about him."

She kept her gaze steady. "You like the dangerous jobs."

"I guess so."

"Your name…"

"I picked Luke Buckley when I needed to disappear."

"Who was the boy who was drowning?"

"My cousin."

"Did you save him?"

"Yeah."

"Where is he now?"

"Married with kids. Let's keep him out of this."

"Okay."

She heard the fatigue in his voice.

"I shouldn't be asking you so many questions. Can you go back to sleep?"

"I hope so. Can you?"

"I should sit in the chair," she murmured. Not because she wanted to drag herself out of bed but because it was the right thing to do.

"Stay here."

After hesitating for a moment, she agreed. "Okay."

She closed her eyes, thinking that sleep would be impossible now. But she was wrong.

IT WAS LATER THE SAME DAY when two men who had never traveled to Louisiana before arrived at the plantation. They parked down the road and walked up toward Cypress Cottage, the place that Liam Bridges had rented from the old lady who owned the place, only in Louisiana he was going by the name Luke Buckley. But that wasn't going to help him now that they knew where he was.

The two wiseguys went by Eddie and Bobby. Not their real names, but good enough for the work they did. Eddie was tall and lean, going bald and in his mid-thirties, but nobody would have dared call attention to his lack of hair. Bobby was a few years younger, but he had the same hardened look.

They waited in the shadows under the trees for signs of life. The old lady who owned the place was dead. Which made things less messy. The lights were out in the big house. Also in Cypress Cottage, but it could be some kind of trap.

Caution was one of the reasons these two men had survived in a rat-eat-rat world.

After checking Boudreaux's car, Bobby crossed the porch and tried the door. It was unlocked, and he nodded at his partner.

Guns drawn, they stepped inside and knew at once that their quarry wasn't at home.

"Looks like he's cleared out," Eddie muttered as he took in the disarray.

"And somebody with feet bigger than Buckley's been here after him. Used his shirt to wipe their muddy shoes."

"What the hell is going on?"

"Don't know. But looky here." Bobby pointed to a fresh bloodstain on the arm of a chair.

"Somebody's wounded."

"Buckley?"

"I'd like to know. Maybe we're not the only ones who got a beef with him."

They kept searching but didn't find anything to indicate where the man they were supposed to kill had gone.

"I guess we'd better have a look in the big house," Eddie said. "Maybe we'll find a lead."

"Yeah, we gotta, cause Maglioni is going to be furious if we come up empty."

They left the cottage and headed for the main plantation house, circling the building and trying the windows. One of them pushed in easily and fell with the clatter of breaking glass onto the basement floor below.

"Another surprise," Bobby observed.

"Maybe nobody's keeping the place up."

"Or the guy with the muddy shoes was here."

"Either way, let's not look a gift horse in the mouth."

They entered cautiously, alert for booby traps.

Once inside the basement, they drew their guns and started for the first floor. A search of the house revealed that nobody was home and there had been some kind of disturbance in an upstairs bedroom.

Eddie pointed toward a bullet hole in the wall. "The plot thickens."

His partner studied the scene. "My guess is that there was an ambush here. They were the winners. They went back to the cottage, cleared out and left in his car."

"So where did they go?"

"She works in New Orleans. Maybe we can get a line on them in the city."

WHEN GABRIELLA WOKE AGAIN, she was gripped by a confusing kaleidoscope of thoughts and sensations. A dull ache had settled in her arm, and at the same time, a wave of desire flooded through her.

Her eyes blinked open, and she stared up into Luke Buckley's face, seeing the mixture of sensations that she'd already picked up from his mind.

He was leaning over her, the hand on his good side caressing her lips.

"Don't," she whispered against his fingers, unable to keep her lips from playing with his finger.

He made another seductive sweep. "You like it."

"I can't hide that from you, but we both know you need to rest."

"Was it part of the dream, or did you get into my nightmare? Did we talk about it?"

"I did—and we talked."

"Strange, don't you think?"

She nodded.

"We need to find out what's going on between us."

It was a simple statement of fact, but it said so much about intimacy on so many different levels. She needed this man. In ways that she hadn't even admitted to herself.

His fingers slipped to her jaw, then the column of her throat, trailing a very agreeable warmth.

"Don't think about him," he said.

"You mean the guy who's trying to kill us?"

"Needle in a haystack."

"Maybe we'd have a better chance if we split up," she murmured.

She didn't have to get inside his mind to feel the tension rippling through him. "Are you kidding?"

"You don't have any obligation to me."

"Are you trying to drive me away?"

Was she? Had she come up with the suggestion because she felt too much? She longed to keep feeling this connection with Luke, but was she also afraid she would lose it? And she couldn't cope with the loss?

"You have to learn to take chances." He answered her unspoken thoughts.

She couldn't hold back a quick reaction. "I do take chances. I bet everything that I could make it as a chef in New Orleans." She gulped. "And now I've lost my job."

His voice rang with outrage. "Because you didn't show up for work?"

"Yes."

"Nice guy."

"I knew that when I signed on as his kitchen slave."

"You'll get a better position. You've got a great reputation. Maybe that's why Emile was so quick to let you go when you gave him an excuse. He knows that people are talking about you more than him. They're probably coming to his restaurant for the desserts."

"You didn't even hear the conversation I had with him, did you? You're getting all that—how?"

"I'm picking up impressions. Reacting to his behavior. Making deductions. That's my job."

As Luke spoke, he leaned over, brushing his lips against hers. She knew he felt the sharp shaft of desire that stabbed through her. His hand drifted down, to the top of her breast, then lower, gliding over her nipple, making it instantly hard.

"Nice," he murmured. "You want me."

"Of course I do. But we can't. You can't."

"Let me be the judge of that."

His voice was so seductive. More seductive was the increased pressure of his mouth against hers, the way his hand slipped under her shirt and stroked across the skin of her belly. Even though her denial made sense, she couldn't stop the heat that suddenly surged through her.

Through them, because his touch let her feel his desire and her own. It was strange to focus on that, on the way a man's body reacted to arousal, with most of the sensations focused in one place.

They had kissed before, touched before. The intensity was more now, building from the previous times.

"Lie down," she whispered against his mouth.

He eased back against the pillows, his hand stroking the hair back from her forehead.

"I'm going to check your arm."

"And here I thought you were seducing me."

"Be serious."

"I am."

"We'll see how you're feeling later."

He sighed, but he didn't stop her as she turned on the bedside lamp and took off the bandage, trying to ignore his heated thoughts. She might be focused on tending to his wound. He was still focused on the erotic possibilities of the moment.

"Men!"

He laughed.

"You're not as steady as you're pretending to be."

"Thanks for the news bulletin."

Trying to focus on something besides her own arousal, she inspected the wound. It looked about the same, which was a good sign, she assumed. No redness. No swelling. As far as she could tell, it wasn't infected. And she knew from his silent assessment as she worked that the pain was less than it had been.

She put on more antiseptic, then used more sterile pads and tied them in place.

"We're going to need to stop at a drugstore," she said. "I'm running out of supplies."

"Later."

"We should eat."

"You're stalling."

"And you're hungry."

He laughed. "And you happen to have food in the trunk. But nothing exactly nourishing. Are your desserts good enough to substitute for sex?"

"I think you said you read the reviews of my work."

"Yes."

She caught another thought from his mind.

"Yes, I brought home goodies for my mom." With the mention of her mother, recent memories zinged back to her.

To distract herself, she climbed off the bed and found her shoes. Outside she looked up at the sky. They'd slept much of the day and into the evening.

It was tempting to bring in a change of clothing, but she could do that later. Leaving the luggage in the car, she picked up the box of desserts.

Luke was sitting up when she came back. After spreading a towel on the bed, she opened the box, revealing a tempting selection.

"No forks. I'm sorry."

"Not to worry. More fun this way." Luke broke a piece off a flourless chocolate cake and ate it. "This is good. It really is almost a substitute for sex."

"Uh-huh." She smiled at him, thinking that this warm interlude was a sample of what she could have with him—if a killer wasn't after them.

Trying to shut that thought out of her mind, she took some of the same cake, then helped herself to part of a pecan pie. It was a spectacularly decadent meal.

Luke licked his fingers. "A nice picnic."

"I could go out and buy something more substantial."

His reaction was instantaneous. Grabbing her wrist, he said, "The guy's looking for you. You can't go out."

Trying to focus on logic rather than reaction, she answered, "We can't stay here forever."

"We'll wait a few hours, then see how things are going."

He was still holding on to her, making the connection between them again.

She should pull away, but she stayed where she was, letting her thoughts drift to his, pleased that she could do it more easily.

"You thought that guy who was trying to kidnap me could be from the mob."

"I changed my mind, but they're still looking for me."

The conversation was quickly being overwhelmed by the desire building between them.

*More than I ever felt before,* he said into her mind, echoing her earlier thought.

"Why is this happening with us?"

"I don't know."

*I keep thinking we can use...it,* Gabriella said.

*How?*

*I wish I knew. I wish I knew how we got it.*

BILL WELLINGTON, ALSO KNOWN as the Badger, carefully replaced the receiver. He'd been waiting for a call from George Camden, and when his operative hadn't checked in, he tried the guy's cell. No answer. Which was probably not good news. If George had his cell turned off, he must be afraid to report his lack of progress.

He clenched his fists, struggling to control his anger. This was the second time in the past month that the hired help hadn't proved up to the job of capturing one of the children from the clinic. Apparently it was what you got when you used guys who had more brawn than brains.

Had Gabriella gotten away because she was with the Buckley guy? Or was it because she had some special talents that Bill didn't know about?

The last couple who'd slipped out of his clutches had both been from the clinic, but there was no record of anyone named Luke Buckley. So who the hell was he, and why was he protecting Gabriella?

Or did he have his own agenda? Which was what? Did he have a line on Gabriella's origins and think he could exploit them in some way?

Wellington sighed. Much as he hated coming out of the shadows, he was beginning to think he'd better go to Louisiana. Then he'd be nearby if Camden managed to round up the girl. If not, he'd have to make other arrangements.

GEORGE CAMDEN SLOWED AS he came to another motel. With no other options, he'd been methodically checking each one in the towns around Lafayette, still assuming that Buckley wasn't getting very far with a bullet wound. George had been to dozens of places, going north first, then coming back toward town and picking another route. This was hopeless, but he had no better options.

Or maybe he could go back to Houma and start over again. Find someone else who had worked at that damn clinic and make them talk. What if he started fresh with a different woman who had gone there so she could have a brat to take care of?

The idea was tempting. Only then he'd have to explain to the Badger why he had failed to scoop up Gabriella Boudreaux. And he had the feeling that the Badger was the type of guy who didn't deal well with failure.

He turned into the parking lot of the Lazy Bayou and

scanned the cars, looking for one covered with mud. He didn't see anything like the swampmobile that had zoomed out of the bayou, but it could be around back.

With a weary sigh, he pulled up at the office and got out.

The clerk behind the counter eyed him as he stepped through the door.

"Help you?"

"I'm looking for a guy."

"That takes in half the human race."

He laughed. "Well, this is a jerk who gave me some trouble last night. Did you get anyone…who was trying to spin you a story?"

"I don't give out that kind of information for free."

George pulled out a fifty dollar bill and pushed it toward the clerk.

The man's hand snaked out and whisked the money out of sight. "I got a guy who said he was alone, but a woman was hiding in the backseat of his car."

George's ears perked up. "Oh, yeah?"

"The guy looked wasted."

GABRIELLA HADN'T SEEN the motel office because Luke had told her to wait in the car. Now a sudden picture of the little room formed in her mind.

She was seeing it from Luke's point of view when he'd been in there pretending that he was in town for a friend's wedding—and that the two of them had gotten sloshed together.

He'd spun out that story, then he'd asked the guy to…

Her focus shifted to the clerk.

The scene leaped forward. The man was talking to… George.

In the next second, the phone rang.

# *Chapter Eight*

Gabriella stared at the ringing phone. She didn't need Luke to tell her what was wrong.

"We have to get out of here," she said. "George was in the motel office."

Luke didn't ask how she knew. He only said, "Check the window."

Gabriella pulled the curtains aside and looked out.

"Too late. A car's coming down the driveway."

It was the same car that had followed them into the swamp.

Luke muttered a curse before picking up the phone and holding the receiver to his ear. "Thanks," he said in a harsh voice, then slammed the receiver down again.

"We've still got the gun, right?" she asked in a strangled voice.

"Yeah, but odds are he has another one by now. And this isn't such a great place for a shoot-out."

"What are we going to do?"

Luke ducked into the bathroom, then charged out again. His face was gray but his voice was firm. "There's a window. You can get out that way."

She gasped. "What about you?"

When he told her what he had in mind, she shook her head. "No. That leaves you in too much danger."

"My specialty. And we don't have time for a debate. Just make sure you close the window behind you so he doesn't know where you went."

Although she wanted to argue, she knew he was right. Still, she couldn't shake a sick feeling as she picked up the gun from the bedside table and headed for the bathroom.

Behind her, she could hear Luke moving around the room, getting ready. She'd hooked up with a man of action, one who had been in tight spots before. If she'd been on her own, George would have captured her at the plantation.

Now Luke had come up with another plan.

Unfortunately, getting out wasn't so easy. The window was stuck.

Teeth gritted, she tried to wrench it upward several times with no results. Should she break it?

No. Then George would know where she'd gone. She gave it one more desperate try, and the sash slid up with a grinding noise.

The opening was small, and she had to step on the toilet tank and wiggle one shoulder out, then the other. Her heart was pounding as she eased through. Before she could make her escape, she heard a sharp rap on the door.

When Luke didn't answer, a hard voice called out, "Open up."

"I can't."

She knew Luke was trying to buy her time. With her heart in her throat, she struggled to close the window behind her. Then she leaned against the building for a moment, trying to catch her breath and steeling herself for what came next.

LUKE LAY BACK ON THE BED, on top of the covers. His shirt was still off, the bandage prominent on his arm where the guy would spot it right away.

He ran a hand through his hair, mussing it as he arranged

his features so he looked as if he was in pain. Which wasn't difficult because the damn arm still hurt. But not as badly as he wanted George to think.

"Open up, damn you!"

The door shook on its hinges and held for a moment longer, then finally burst open. The man who had shot him plowed into the room. He had a determined expression on his face and a gun in his hand. Luke's gun, the one he'd left at the cottage. Too bad he hadn't been thinking straight when he'd cleared out.

"Where is she?" the intruder asked.

"Not here," he said in a thin voice, trying to convey the impression that he was on his last legs.

The guy kept the gun trained on Luke as he opened the closet and checked inside, then looked into the bathroom.

"Where is she?" he said again.

Luke stared at him. "Leave me alone. I'm hurt."

The guy gave him a calculating look. "Tough luck. I guess you were in the wrong place at the wrong time."

Well, that was an interesting piece of information. Proof positive that Luke had not been the target.

"What did you want with her, George?" he asked, trying out the name.

The guy's eyes bugged out. "How did you…"

"Trade secret."

The man took a step forward.

Luke kept his gaze focused on George, even when he saw movement in back of him.

He couldn't keep from reacting. He'd expected to see Gabriella running into the bayou. Instead, he saw the motel clerk coming toward the room. Apparently he hadn't been able to leave well enough alone. Probably he was thinking there would be entertainment value in the confrontation. But even as the clerk entered the room, he saw Gabriella through the window, coming toward the doorway.

Luke swore.

The clerk stood paralyzed.

They'd agreed that Gabriella would get the hell out of there. Now a sick feeling tore through Luke as he watched her rushing toward what could be disaster. She must have agreed to his plan only because she had plans of her own. And now the clerk was gumming them up.

In his mind he shouted to her, *Get back. Get out of here.*

*But you...*

*Get back!*

They were talking to each other without speaking. They'd done it before, when they'd been touching. Now it seemed the danger had forged the link even when they were yards apart. But he didn't have time to marvel at the new development. Too much was happening.

George whirled, confronting the clerk. "Keep your nose out of this."

The nosy guy was backing away.

Then to Luke's horror, Gabriella moved closer.

"No!" Luke shouted, watching his hasty plan falling apart in front of his eyes.

George wavered as he spotted Gabriella. When he pointed the gun toward her, Luke pulled his good hand from under the covers. He was holding a knife, and he threw it toward George. He was aiming for the center of the guy's back, but his hand wasn't as steady as it could be, and he hit the side of his back.

Luke cursed, but he'd obviously done some damage.

George screamed and staggered back, hitting the chair and pitching backward onto the floor, the knife going in deeper. He also squeezed the trigger, but the bullet plowed into the wall.

Although Luke had leaped out of bed, he wasn't in tip-top shape. As he changed rapidly from horizontal to vertical, he had to fight a wave of dizziness at the sudden movement.

The clerk was blubbering, staring wide-eyed at the totally unexpected action around him like a man who had wandered into a war zone. The guy with the knife in his shoulder was trying to figure out who to shoot.

"No!" Luke shouted as Gabriella charged toward George. She kept coming and stamped on the hand with the gun—hard.

George screamed again as her foot ground into his palm.

The move had given Luke precious seconds.

Still he had to steady himself before snatching a lamp from the table, yanking the cord free as he barreled toward the gunman. With force born of blinding rage, he brought down the makeshift club on the guy's head. George made a strangled sound and went still.

"What the hell?" the clerk shouted, staring around him as though unable to believe any of what had just happened.

"Call the police," Luke said. "This guy tried to kill us yesterday."

"But you told me…"

"A story. Because we were hiding out from him."

"He was robbing my mom's house," Gabriella added. "We caught him in the act, and he attacked us. But we got away."

Luke was thinking it didn't all make perfect sense as he pulled on the shoes he'd left beside the bed. Still shirtless, he stepped out the door.

"Wait!" the clerk shouted. "You can't leave."

"Watch us."

"You've got to talk to the cops."

"No." He turned to Gabriella. "Get in the car and start the engine."

She stared at him, wide-eyed. “Your shirt.”

“Later.”

When she hesitated, he closed his hand around her arm, trying to convey his urgency with silent words. *No time to try and explain. We have to get away.*

She gave him a little nod, then left the room and crossed to the vehicle.

When she’d climbed behind the wheel, Luke focused on the clerk again. “You were right here and saw the whole thing. Tell them what happened. And I’d cover him with the gun, in case he wakes up. Tell the cops his name is George.”

As Gabriella started to pull out, Luke reconsidered his strategy, just in case George became functional. “Wait.”

He took the gun they’d acquired the day before, leaned out the window and shot two of the tires on George’s vehicle, then shot at the engine block. When he pulled the trigger again, the gun clicked, and he made a face.

“Empty.”

“But he’s not leaving anytime soon,” she answered as Luke leaned back against the seat.

“Go.”

“Where?”

He hadn’t planned that far ahead. All he could say was, “Away. Don’t speed.”

As she drove toward town, he heard a police siren and cursed.

“What should I do?” Gabriella asked.

“Keep going like you’re minding your own business.”

She did, at a steady pace, and the cop car sped past them with lights flashing.

“They don’t know it’s us.”

“Right.”

He leaned back and closed his eyes. When he felt the vehicle turn and slow, he sat up and looked around.

They were on a narrow road shaded by cypress trees.

Gabriella pulled onto the shoulder and cut the engine.

"What?"

She gestured toward his bare chest. "You should put on a shirt."

He laughed. "Yeah."

He climbed out, opened the back door and reached for the bag he was glad he hadn't brought into the motel. He had one more long-sleeved shirt. He'd have to get some more.

Standing on the road, he buttoned the front, then tucked in the tails, glad that the action only caused minor pain.

When he climbed back into the car, he saw Gabriella was shaking. Saw her skin was pale and her features drawn.

"Luke," she said in a barely audible voice.

A wealth of emotions welled up inside him.

He reached for her, and she came into his arms. He felt her fear, her relief, her confusion. And everything else that came with the contact.

"Why didn't you get out of there?" Luke asked.

"I couldn't leave you. I didn't know if you had the strength to throw the knife." She gazed up at him. "But you were so steady. Weren't you…scared?"

"You have to block the fear and do what you have to."

She nodded, and he folded her close again.

"We…we…talked in our minds—when he was going to shoot."

"I noticed."

"Always before it was when we were touching, but we weren't touching then."

"It must have been the danger. It must have juiced up the…connection between us."

"I thought we could use…the talent. I didn't know how."

His hands slid restlessly up and down her back, and hers moved over him in the same jerky rhythm.

He closed his eyes, blocking out everything but the woman in his arms, feeling desire build between them again. And feeling the mental bond between them strengthen. He couldn't explain it. He only knew it existed. And it was pulling them closer together every time they touched. It made him crave her.

But it wasn't all good. He sensed that, sensed the edge of danger as her mind opened to his and his to hers. His head was pounding, and the only way to ignore the pain was to lower his mouth to hers.

His lips moved against hers, the kisses turning hard and insistent as he told her how much he wanted her. Not just with his hands and mouth but in her mind.

*Oh, yes,* she answered as she kissed him just as greedily. They could have died back there at the motel. But they had saved themselves.

They clung together, celebrating their escape, celebrating what was to come. Yet the pain in his head was as insistent as his arousal.

She wrenched her mouth away. "We have to stop."

"Why?"

"This is a bad place to…try something new. We're parked in a car on a one-lane road. In broad daylight. Somebody could come along."

"Details."

He eased away from her, and she stared at him. "Does your head hurt?"

"Yes."

"Mine, too. What does it mean?"

"Maybe that the mental stuff builds up…pressure."

"And I think we can deal with it better…somewhere private."

He laughed. "Yeah, like a nice bedroom."

"Where?"

"I'm thinking the best place to get lost is in the city."

"Okay."

"But not your apartment."

"You think…George is still going to be after us?" she asked as she started the car, then found a place to turn around.

"I don't know, but I think we have to work under the assumption that he is—until we get confirmation that he can't get to us."

She dragged in a breath and let it out. "I'd like to assume we're safe, but I think you're right."

"His name really is George."

"How do you know?"

"I called him that. He was astonished—and angry."

"Score one for us."

As they drove back toward New Orleans, he tried to think about their situation from all angles, and he didn't like the conclusions he was forming.

Finally, he said, "We can't use credit cards. That's going to be a problem at any big hotel chain."

"Why?"

"He could trace your name. And he knows my alias, too."

"How?"

"I guess he checked me out before he went after your mom."

She took her eyes from the road for a moment and studied him. "Where did you learn to think like a criminal?"

"By writing about them."

He could see her trying to come up with a plan. If he reached for her, he might find out what was churning in her mind, but in his present condition, he thought it might be better to keep his hands to himself.

"I know an apartment we can use," she said.

"Whose?"

"Emily Philips, one of the restaurant staffers, is out of town. She won't mind if we use her place."

"You're sure?"

"She's thinking about moving to another city, and we talked about her maybe subletting it to me. If she moves, I'd be doing her a favor. She said I could stay there and see how I liked it."

"You've already got a place."

"This would be a step up."

"Okay."

She kept driving toward the city, into the edge of the French Quarter near the French Market, which was a few blocks from Emile's restaurant.

"How are we going to get in?"

"Her key is on top of the door frame."

"Not very secure."

"I assume George isn't there waiting for us."

"Yeah. Not unless he got away from the local cops and got his knife wound treated. Also, probably a concussion."

She winced. "I didn't even know you had a knife before we figured out that escape plan at the motel."

"It makes a nice silent weapon."

"If you know how to use it."

"We're leaving a trail of destruction behind us. Like that motel lamp."

"We'll take care of that when we're in the clear," he answered.

"If we ever are."

"Have faith. Right now our job is to get off the street. What if Emile saw you?"

She laughed. "Maybe he'd go after me with one of the kitchen knives. He's had plenty of practice cutting up chickens."

"You're no chicken."

She drove around in back of the pastel green stucco building to the alley and parked in an empty slot. Then she led him to the back door of a small apartment building. Inside, they climbed to the second floor, where she went to one of the units and felt along the top of the door frame until she found a key. "See?"

Inside, she started to call her friend's name, but Luke put a restraining hand on her arm.

"Wait here."

He walked through the rooms, gun in hand, checking closets and behind furniture. They were out of bullets, but the weapon would intimidate anyone he encountered.

It was a large apartment with a living room/dining room combination open to the kitchen, a bathroom and a bedroom. The furnishings looked as if they could have been collected from various flea markets, but it was put together with charm. All in all, a pretty good place to hide out.

And clearly George wasn't waiting for them.

GEORGE CAMDEN HAD HIS own problems at the moment. The good news was that he wasn't in a jail cell. Instead, when he opened his eyes, he saw a bunch of hospital monitoring equipment.

Nice of the cops to take him here. Where he could escape, as soon as he had enough strength. Because for the moment he was feeling like crap.

That jerk Luke Buckley had gotten the drop on him by bringing a knife to a gunfight. George would have laughed at the old joke, except that the joke was on him.

It had turned out to be the right move, a nasty surprise for George, but Buckley was also wounded. Which counted for something on their personal score sheet. Although obviously he hadn't been in as bad shape as he'd been pretending at the beginning.

His musings were interrupted when the door opened and a nurse came in, followed by a cop. George looked at the guy through slitted eyes, pretending he was still out of it while he got the lay of the land.

One cop. Was there another in the hall?

The nurse checked his vital signs, and he groaned when she turned him so she could change his bandage. It hurt like hell. He needed a smoke to calm his nerves, but he sure wasn't going to get one here.

His head felt fuzzy. Probably they'd given him something for the pain. Which was good for the time being, but he'd have to get off the meds before he made his escape.

As he listened to the cop and the nurse talking, he realized he had an advantage. Nobody was absolutely sure what had happened back at the motel. Gabriella and Buckley might be in the wrong. They'd certainly registered under an assumed name, and their story had been hinkey.

When the motel clerk had asked them to hang around, they'd fled, which made them look guilty of *something.*

George hadn't been carrying identification, so the cops didn't know who *he* was at all. At least not yet. If they'd checked his fingerprints, the information hadn't come back yet. But how much time did he have before they nailed him?

When the nurse and the cop left, he tried to get comfortable. For the moment, the whole incident presented a nice little puzzle for the Podunk Police Department. His mind started scrambling. Maybe he could spin some kind of story that would get him out of here—as soon as he was well enough to travel.

Of course, he didn't know exactly where Gabriella and Buckley had gone, but he figured they didn't have too many options. Houma was probably a good bet, unless they had enough cash to get out of the country.

# *Chapter Nine*

In the bedroom, Luke turned around to find Gabriella standing behind him.

"Put down the gun," she said, her voice not quite steady.

They had known each other only for days, but it might as well have been a lifetime. Getting inside each other's minds had been a shortcut to intimacy. So had the danger swirling around them.

They had been on the verge of making love before, but it had never been the right time. Now it was.

When he reached for her, she came into his arms, sighing as her body pressed against his.

A question circled in her mind. *You're sure you're okay?*

"Yeah, better than okay. Now."

He knew she caught all the wealth of meaning below the surface of the words, knew she was tuned to him in a way he didn't understand. But he also knew they had crossed some kind of barrier that had always separated them from the rest of humanity. A whole new world was open to them.

Yet they were both nervous about taking the next step because they were leaping off into the unknown.

*Together,* she reminded him, then spoke aloud, "This is better than that dismal motel room for the first time we make love."

He didn't have to say anything to give her his agreement. She knew they were on the same wavelength.

In the car, after they'd escaped from the motel, their kisses had been frantic. He didn't want it to be that way now. He wanted this to be slow—perfect.

"It will be," she answered.

He lowered his head. She raised hers, and their lips met. He wanted it to be gentle, and he managed to keep it that way, but below the movement of his lips against hers, he felt passion building.

When they came up for air, they were both trembling.

"You need to get off your feet," she murmured.

"We will."

They both walked toward the bed in the center of the room. She crossed to the far side, and together they turned down the covers.

When she came back to him, he gave her a warm look. Again, he knew she followed his thoughts. He didn't want to touch her. Not yet.

Boldly she pulled her shirt over her head and unhooked her bra.

He caught his breath as she tossed it away, revealing her gorgeous breasts.

His mouth was so dry he could barely speak, but he managed to say, "You are so beautiful."

"I want to be. For you."

He pulled off his shirt, wincing when he had to move his arm.

When she started to speak, he shook his head. "Nothing is going to stop us this time."

"When I was bandaging your arm, I didn't tell you how much I love your chest. It's so nice and broad. If I'm beautiful, so are you."

"You don't mind chest hair?"

"It's part of the appeal for me. I'm going to enjoy the way it feels."

The comment made his mouth go even dryer. "Against your breasts?" he asked, his voice thick.

"Yes. And my fingers," she answered with a smile that made the blood pump hotly through his veins.

They were both in a hurry, but neither one of them was going to rush. When she reached for the button at the top of her pants, he did, too. He undid his belt, lowered his zipper, watching her as she did the same, then pulled down her slacks and panties at the same time.

He kept his gaze on her body as he slicked his pants down his legs, doing the same thing she had—getting rid of the rest of his clothing quickly.

He watched her take in his body and the erection standing out with serious intent.

She smiled. "You're in good shape."

"Except for a little problem with my arm."

They were teasing each other, building up the level of heat without touching. But it was more than teasing.

He grinned at her, then felt his expression turn serious as he reached for her.

She came into his arms, the shock of naked skin to naked skin almost taking his breath away. With a gasp, she wrapped her arms around him, clinging to him to hold on to her sanity.

That was a strange way to put it, but he knew it was true.

The pressure in his head was back. Only now it felt as if some animal with claws was inside his skull, trying to dig its way out.

He shuddered at the image, and might have thrust her away from him, but he understood that if they lost their nerve and let go of each other now, it would be worse, much worse. The only way to cope was to see this through.

His whole body was tingling. No, it was her body. That was the way a woman felt when she was aroused.

When she closed her hand around his erection, his breath caught. So did hers as she melted into the sensations she was picking up from him.

"Oh, that's good," she murmured. So different. So focused there.

He admired her ability to speak. He was beyond speech. Beyond anything that he had ever felt.

His own arousal. Hers. The incredible heat they generated together.

They broke apart long enough to stagger to the bed, where they fell together, clinging, rocking, absorbing each other's needs and thoughts.

He was totally open to her. More vulnerable than he ever had been in his life. If he had murdered someone in the past, she would have known it. If he had been dishonest in any of his writing; if he had copied someone else's words, she would know it.

And it was the same for her. She tried to pull away when he came upon the memory of the first time she had made love. It had been a disaster.

*Trust me. This time will be so different.*

*I think we have to trust each other.*

He held her to him, overwhelmed with what she offered as he told her in every way he knew that this would be wonderful. It already was wonderful. And growing more intense as he stroked her breasts, her ribs, the indentation of her waist, the insides of her thighs and higher, reaching for that throbbing place that begged for his touch.

He knew just how to do it. Just how to stoke her pleasure. Just how to push her toward the edge because he registered every reaction.

The look in her eyes scalded him.

*I need you inside me.*

He needed that, too. And he knew she was thinking that it would be better for his arm if she were on top.

Their eyes locked as he lay back and she rose over him, bringing him inside her, each of them totally committed to something they didn't yet understand. But it would consume them if they were unable to control it.

They both gasped at the joining. For long moments, neither of them moved. Finally she surged against him, and he thrust farther into her at the same time.

Together they found a rhythm that would take them into outer space. But was the air above the earth too thin to breathe?

Her gaze stayed locked with his as the intensity built. For a terrifying moment, the pain in his head surged. In hers, too, he knew. It threatened to wipe out everything else. The pleasure they felt. Life itself.

Then blessed relief washed over them as the pain receded into the background. The foreground was far more important. The two of them, giving each other pleasure.

Knowing she needed an extra jolt to push her over the edge, he reached up with one hand, pressing against her center.

As she moved above him, an explosion built, flashing through her, flashing through him. Her orgasm was his. And his was hers as he followed her into an ecstasy that he had never known existed.

They clung together for long moments, both panting, both marveling at what had just happened.

*I was alone all my life.*

*Never again.*

*How did it happen?*

*We'll figure it out.*

*Can we?*

*Yes.* It was a promise that he must keep.

A question hovered at the edge of her mind, a question she didn't want to ask. But it was there for him to consider anyway.

*Did we almost die?*

He swallowed hard. *I think so.*

*What saved us?*

I don't know.

"Maybe it was what I said, being willing to trust each other." She swallowed. "And giving each other everything we could."

He stroked her arm. "That sounds right."

When she slipped down beside him, he cradled her in his good arm.

She snuggled against him, and he knew she felt safe and secure. But he knew it was a false security. They were still in trouble.

FAR AWAY, RACHEL GREGORY stirred in her sleep. Next to her, Jake Harper knit his fingers with hers. A month ago she'd been a tarot card reader in New Orleans with her own shop. Jake had been a prominent businessman in the city who had worked his way up from nothing.

They'd met each other and known instantly that there was something between them that they couldn't explain. A psychic bond triggered by intimacy.

But as they'd explored that special connection, they'd been pulled into a web of danger by a woman named Evelyn Morgan. She'd come to New Orleans looking for them because they had both been born as the result of experiments at the Solomon Clinic in Houma, Louisiana.

The psychic connection they'd discovered was wonderful. It brought them joy neither had ever imagined.

At the same time, the dangers had multiplied around them.

They'd been on the run from the police and from a man who knew something about the clinic. But that had only been part of their problem. A couple named Tanya and Mickey had realized Rachel and Jake were developing mental powers and had been determined to kill them before they could cement their bond.

They'd dealt with Tanya and Mickey, but they were still hiding out from the man who had funded the Solomon Clinic, a man they knew only as the Badger. Until they could find him and get him off their trail, it wasn't safe for them to resume their normal lives.

In the meantime, they'd been working with the psychic link between them, trying to increase their abilities and their safety.

Rachel woke, hearing Jake's voice in her mind.

*What is it?* he asked.

*I felt something.*

*Danger? Has the Badger found us?*

*I don't think so. I think another couple like us has found each other.*

*And activated the bond?*

*I think so.*

Rachel lay very still, sending her mind across the miles. She knew the right direction, toward New Orleans—where it had all started for them.

*If we were closer, it would be easier to figure out what's going on.*

*Yeah, well, we're not going back there. Not until we know it's safe.*

*But I think they're in trouble. The way we were,* she answered, feeling a tightness in her chest.

Jake squeezed her hand. "And you want to help them."

"Yes."

"But suppose they're like Tanya and Mickey? Suppose they come after us?"

She sighed. "I don't know."

"We'd better be a little cautious. Wait and see."

"I think they just…made love. For the first time."

"And they survived?"

"Yes."

She knew he was right to be cautious, yet after what she and Jake had been through, the idea of letting two people like them suffer alone was almost more than she could bear.

GEORGE CAMDEN HAD FIGURED out how to escape. He'd played it cagey when the cops had come back to question him, pretending he was so traumatized that he couldn't remember what had happened in that motel room. He wasn't sure if the boys in blue completely bought it, but there was no proof he'd done anything besides defend himself.

Still, he had to be careful. At two in the morning, he detached his intravenous line, then looked out of his room. The guard at the door was sleeping. Quietly, George slipped out and hurried down the hall—prepared to act confused if anybody challenged him.

He stepped into a double room where two men were sleeping in hospital beds. Although he struck out with the first guy's nightstand, in the second one he found a cell phone and called the man who'd hired him.

The Badger picked up on the first ring.

"Who is this?"

"George Camden."

"This isn't your phone."

No bull. "I ran into a little trouble."

The man's voice was instantly on edge. "Is that why I haven't heard from you?"

"Yes. I'm in the hospital in Lafayette. I need your help to get out."

"I'm listening."

"How long will it take you to get here?"

"Not long. I'm in New Orleans."

"You are?"

"I thought I might need to take personal charge of the operation."

Was the Badger being down here good or bad? Maybe not so good for George. Maybe he'd better get out of here before the guy arrived.

"We'd better wait until tomorrow night," he said, changing his plans on the spur of the moment.

"Why?"

"I got knifed. I'm weak."

"Okay. Can you meet me at the back entrance. At 2:00 a.m. tomorrow?"

"Yes," he answered, scrambling for a way to skip out sooner.

EXHAUSTED FROM THEIR eventful day, Gabriella and Luke slept, then woke early in the morning, drifting in the world of their new reality.

She turned her head, smiling at him. He reached for her hand under the covers and linked his fingers with hers.

*I don't even know what to call you,* she said into his mind. *Luke? Liam?*

He stroked her arm. *You like Luke because you knew it first.*

*Yes.*

*Keep using it. It belongs to us.*

It was tempting to stay where they were. Tempting to enjoy the unique sense of closeness. But they had work to do. And too many choices.

"We'd better get up," she said.

"Unfortunately."

She looked toward the kitchen. "I think there's coffee. And creamer."

He wrinkled his nose. "It's much better black."

She started to get out of bed, then realized she was naked.

"I've seen it all," he murmured.

"I'm still modest."

"I know."

He got up and handed her the clothing she'd worn the night before. She pulled on the shirt while she sat in bed.

When she looked up, he was holding out clean underwear from her overnight bag, and she knew he'd read her mind about that.

*Convenient!*

*Mind to mind communication has its advantages.*

She switched to spoken language. "We could shower."

"Good idea."

The shower turned into more than an exercise in getting clean. An hour later, they were finally sitting at a small table in front of the window drinking coffee and eating cheese and crackers they'd found in the cupboard and refrigerator.

"Is our mental connection just for communication?" Gabriella asked as she took a sip of coffee.

"Not if you consider fiction," he said. "Or the movies. Did you read a lot of science fiction when you were little? Or fantasy?"

"Yes. I loved it when people could talk to each other without speaking."

"Because you wanted it?"

"Well, it was a strong fantasy of mine."

It was tempting to keep talking about the past, but they

couldn't afford the luxury. Gabriella huffed out a breath before saying, "When George was after us, we used the communication to defend ourselves."

He nodded. "What else could they do in the stories you read?"

She thought for a moment. "See the future. We can already do that—a little." She swallowed. "Like when I knew I was going to find something bad back at the plantation. Or I knew George had found us at the motel."

He reached for her hand and squeezed it. "Yes."

"In books, some people can also see the past."

"Maybe that's not as useful in this situation. What about my getting into your dreams. Does that count?"

"It has to. How many people share dreams?"

She laughed. "I guess not many. Which brings up some leading questions. For instance—are there other people like us? How did we get this way?"

"We've got to find out. But let's keep cataloguing our powers."

"Powers! Like superheroes?"

He shrugged.

She grinned at him. "I've read about people who could walk through walls."

"Sounds painful."

"How about throwing thunderbolts?"

"I'd like that. But what about trying something easier?"

"We could try channeling Elvis Presley's ghost."

He laughed. "Oh, sure. And remember, a lot people think he's not dead anyway. How about something a little more practical, like—um—moving things with our minds."

She nodded. "I'm game."

"I'm assuming we have to be touching."

"At least at first."

EDDIE AND BOBBY DROVE slowly past Chez Emile, taking in the freshly painted entrance and scrubbed brick sidewalk.

"Classy place," Bobby said.

"Do you think we'll find Gabriella Boudreaux?"

"It's our best lead. If she's not there, maybe somebody inside knows where she went."

"How do we pry it out of them? Start shooting them one at a time if they don't talk?"

"Let's try charm first. And money. Money is always good, and Maglioni gave us enough to spread around."

They were in a chipper mood when they found a parking place and walked back to the restaurant.

"We won't be open until lunchtime," a tubby old guy said when they stepped through the front door. He gave them a stare that said they might not be high class enough for this joint, even when it was open.

Eddie wanted to teach the jerk it wasn't polite to insult potential customers. Bobby put a restraining hand on his sleeve. "We're looking for Gabriella Boudreaux. Is she here?"

The guy's face grew tense when they mentioned her name. Interesting. It appeared he wasn't too happy with Ms. Boudreaux.

"What's this about?"

"Private matter."

"She's not here. Her mother died, and she's gone back to Lafayette."

"She's not there now."

The guy gave them a thunderous look. "Not there! She told me..." He stopped short and crossed his arms. "I don't have to explain anything to you."

Bobby got out his wallet. "We're prepared to pay for information."

The man sniffed. "I don't take money for information." He turned away dismissively.

Bobby kept his temper in check. He could whack this jerk, but that wasn't going to get him far. Instead, he looked around, located the door to the kitchen and headed in that direction.

"Hey, you can't go back there!"

"We'll only be a moment," Eddie called over his shoulder.

People in the kitchen looked up as the two strangers entered.

"Family emergency. Anybody know where we can find Gabriella Boudreaux?"

There were shakes of the head and negative answers all around. But one woman looked less certain than the rest.

Bobby approached her, smiling. "Come on outside where we can talk."

She hesitated for a moment, then followed him into the alley out back where trash cans were ripe with rotting garbage. She gave him a questioning look. "What do you want with Gabriella?"

"It's about her mother. You know she died?"

"Yes."

"I need to give her some stuff for the memorial service. Please, if you can tell me where to find her, I can make it worth your while."

"Well…I might have an idea."

LUKE MOVED HIS CHAIR BESIDE Gabriella and slung his arm over her shoulder. They both looked around the room contemplating what they might try to move.

"We could break something if we do it wrong," she murmured.

"We'll be careful."

"I'll hold you to that."

He stood up and put his paper napkin on the floor about

ten feet from where they were sitting. "This should be safe enough."

When he came back and replaced his arm around her, she leaned against him. "What should we do?"

"Both focus on it. Try to make it jump into the air."

"And fly around the room?"

"Let's see if we can get it off the floor first."

She gave him a warm look. She'd never considered herself playful, but she knew they were both having a good time. With a serious purpose.

Unsure of how to proceed, she focused on the napkin, trying to make it move. Nothing happened, and she redoubled her efforts, her face scrunching with effort. Even so, there was no effect.

"What are we doing wrong?" she asked.

"Maybe we're both trying to move it, and we're fighting each other."

"Hum."

"You try to do the moving, and I'll give you a power assist."

"How do you do that?"

He shrugged. "I guess I'll find out."

He leaned against her and closed his eyes, taking his focus off the napkin—which left her free to do what she wanted.

Power assist? Did she feel a tingling sensation? Or was she making that up because she wanted some reaction?

There was no way to know, as she focused intently on the object. Suddenly, to her astonishment, it gave a little leap and fluttered a few inches into the air as though a puff of wind had caught it.

When she gasped, Luke's eyes flew open in time to see the white square flutter to the floor.

"All right!"

His exclamation had her smiling.

Because he was a guy, he needed to try something more difficult. After scanning the bookshelves, he grabbed a paperback mystery and put it where the napkin had been.

She let him take charge and tried what he had done, sending energy to him. To her amazement, the book skittered across the floor. Then he gave it a jolt and made it crash into the wall.

They grinned at each other.

"What else should we try?"

"Too bad we can't do something practical like making the bed without touching the covers."

"You're looking for a way to get out of housework?"

He shrugged. "Why not?"

"Automatic dishwashing?"

"First we have to turn the water on in the sink."

That proved to be a harder proposition, although he did manage to get a trickle to drip out.

All the mental activity was tiring.

"We should knock it off for a while," Luke said.

"Or think of some other parlor tricks."

"They're not just tricks. What if we'd been able to get George to shoot himself?"

"That's not quite the same thing as moving objects with your mind. I'd call that forcing someone to take an action against his best interest. Or that he hadn't planned."

"That would be useful."

She shook her head. "I don't think we can practice that kind of thing on each other. Maybe we should work on the other part of the problem."

"You mean trying to figure out how we got this way?"

"Yes."

"I'll go get the papers you took from your mom's."

As soon as he said it, she felt her stomach knot. There was

something in those papers that she was going to find. And did she want him here when she did?

She tried to shove that thought far down in her mind and focused on her other worry. At the moment, the idea of letting him out of her sight felt wrong.

"Go on," she said. "And hurry back."

## *Chapter Ten*

When Luke left the apartment, Gabriella walked restlessly from the front windows to the back, then to the street side again, staring out at the sidewalk and buildings. When she didn't see anything unusual, she got out her cell phone and found there were two messages from her friend at the restaurant, Tim.

As soon as she heard his voice, she knew something was wrong.

"Gabriella, where are you? There were two tough-looking guys here looking for you. Emile said you'd gone home, but they said you weren't there. Then they started asking people if they knew where you might be. At first nobody would say anything. When they started offering cash for information, Janie went outside with them. I listened in. She remembered that you'd wanted to sublet Emily Philips's apartment. If you're over there, you might want to watch out for them."

She wished she could describe George to Tim and ask if George might have been one of the men. But there might not be time for that. And if it was George, he had someone else with him.

Gabriella took her lower lip between her teeth. She'd suggested this apartment because she'd thought she and Luke would be safe here.

Now it seemed like a very bad idea.

Luke had gone down to the car to get the stuff from her mom. He was outside. And vulnerable.

Her heart was in her throat as she ran to the back window and looked out. Luke was standing beside the car, and two men were on either side of him, both holding guns. Neither one of them was George. Were they mobsters from New Jersey?

She made a muffled sound as her heart began to race. What was she going to do?

In a panic, she tried to reach out to Luke with her mind the way he'd done with her at the motel when George had been standing over him with a gun. At first it was like sending a feeble flashlight beam into a vast, lightless cave. Then she felt a glimmer of something.

*Luke.*

*Thank God. I've been trying to contact you.*

*Tim called me from the restaurant. He said two guys were looking for me.*

*They were using you to get to me. They're from the mob.* He confirmed her suspicion. Even in her mind, she heard the grating quality of his voice and gasped.

*What are we going to do?*

*They don't want any witnesses. They're marching me upstairs. Get out of there.*

*No!* The reaction was automatic. Then she reconsidered. If she were in the apartment, they'd both be trapped.

Too bad Luke had used up the last bullets in George's gun. Or maybe it didn't matter. Probably she couldn't win a gunfight with two experienced thugs.

Better to do something totally unexpected.

Frantically she looked around and found a collection of decorative paperweights on the desk. Snatching up a cluster of them, she ran out the door, closing and locking it behind her, then ran up the steps to the next floor.

Downstairs, she heard Luke and the men come in.

"Hurry up," one of them growled, "or I'll shoot you right here."

He started climbing the steps.

*Luke, I'm on the next floor, in back of you. I locked the door. I'm going to hit the bald one with a paperweight.*

She heard his silent curse echo in her mind.

Her heart was pounding as they came into view. As a kid, she'd thrown stones into the bayou. Now she was thinking that maybe she could add power to her throw by using the technique they had practiced with the napkin and the paperback book.

*Send me your energy,* she asked Luke, hoping he'd heard her.

From her vantage point, she watched him nod slightly as the trio stopped at the door.

"It's locked," the bald one said.

"Oh, well," Luke answered.

"I don't need any smart comments from you."

"Did it ever occur to your boss that I might have duplicate copies of my research, with directions to publish it if anything happens to me?"

"Maybe. But who's going to be stupid enough to do that if you're dead?"

"You might be surprised."

*Now!*

Focused on the man's bald head, Gabriella threw the paperweight. It shot through the air with more force than she could have mustered on her own, finding its mark and hitting with a satisfying thunk.

As the missile struck home, Luke lunged back, grabbing the other man and slamming him into the first.

Gabriella was ready with another paperweight, which she lobbed at the second man. But it went wild, and the guy wrenched himself away from Luke, gun raised.

"Don't shoot," she shouted.

The guy whirled around and spotted her on the steps. She ducked back as he pulled the trigger, feeling a slug travel past her face.

Luke sprang at the man, going for the gun. As they struggled, the first man stirred and started to rise.

She pounded down the stairs, a paperweight in each hand. She clunked the first one down on the guy she'd initially hit, and he went still. Then she turned toward the two men struggling. Luke and Blondie.

She wanted to hit the mob guy, but he and Luke were moving too fast for her to get a clear shot.

Could she affect the fight with her mind? Did she have the energy?

Luke and Blondie were standing on the landing, and she saw that the guy's foot was at the edge of a step.

*I'm going to try for his foot,* she told Luke, hoping the message would get through.

She gathered all her power, pushing at the foot. It seemed she couldn't do anything by herself. Still, she tried harder and saw the shoe inch toward the edge.

It was enough for the guy to waver on his feet. Luke gave him a shove, and he went sailing down the stairs, screaming as the gun went flying and he crashed to the bottom.

Luke ran after him, grabbing the gun and bashing it onto his assailant's head.

The bald one was still on the landing outside the apartment groaning. She hit him again, thinking that his head must be made of iron as the paperweight thunked against his thick skull.

Luke rushed back to her. "Are you all right?"

"Yes. Are you?"

"Yeah. But we've got to get out of here."

"I'm sorry. I thought we'd be okay in Emily's apartment."

"My fault. I didn't even know they were in the area, but they must have tracked me to the plantation."

"And they found you through me. Then they came to the restaurant looking for me, and Janie said I might be here. So let's not assign blame."

He stood with one of the wiseguy's guns at the top of the steps where he could watch both men. "Get our stuff. We're leaving."

She dashed back into the apartment, sweeping what they'd unpacked into their travel bags. She looked around, thinking she should straighten up, but there was no time for that now.

In under two minutes, she was back on the landing. Neither of the men had moved.

TENSION ZINGED THROUGH LUKE as he riffled through the pockets of the guy who had fired at Gabriella. He had never been so scared in his life. Not for himself. For her. The George guy had wanted information from her. These men wanted her dead—so she couldn't talk about him.

He pulled out the man's wallet and keys, then stood. "Come on."

They hurried down the stairs where he searched the second wiseguy and took a second wallet.

"Yeah, it's stealing," he muttered in response to Gabriella's unspoken thought. "Better than murder. Besides, they owe us."

He caught her agreement and her hope that they'd gotten enough money to do them some good. From the size of the wads of bills, it felt as if they'd liberated a small fortune. Unless they were carrying around bricks of ones to tip bellboys.

She laughed, and he knew she'd picked up that thought, too.

After throwing the bags into the back of his car, she looked up to find him unlocking the door of the other vehicle.

"What?"

"I'm going to drive their car away from here, so they can't

come after us. You follow me," he said, when what he really wanted was to reach for her and pull her into his arms—and hold on to her for a long time. But if the guys in there woke up before he and Gabriella left, they were in trouble.

"Where are we going?" she asked.

Good question. "You know the city better than I do. Got a suggestion where I can leave their car where nobody will pay attention to it for a while?"

FAR AWAY, RACHEL WAS MAKING lunch when she went absolutely still.

Jake was immediately on the alert. "What?"

"They're in trouble."

"The other couple you were talking about?"

"Yes."

"The same kind of trouble we were in?"

"I don't know. They were fighting with two men."

"And?"

"I think they got away. But…"

Although she didn't finish the sentence, Jake was becoming an expert at following her thoughts.

"You still want to help them."

"Yes."

"You know that could be dangerous."

"I don't think they're like Mickey and Tanya."

"Why?"

"The best I can tell you is—intuition. I spent a lot of time as a tarot card reader making assessments of people."

"And you'd bet our lives on that now?"

She gave him a pleading look. "They need help."

He sighed. "Where are they?"

"I don't know exactly. Somewhere in the city, but I think they're leaving. I think we need to wait until they get where they're going." She leaned back and closed her eyes, trying to learn more.

LUKE FOLLOWED GABRIELLA as they drove to the old Jax Brewery building that had been converted into a tourist shopping mall.

In the parking lot, he found a space for the thugs' vehicle, then climbed back into his car. They exchanged a long look, but neither one of them wanted to linger.

Gabriella exited, paying a minimal fee for the few minutes they'd been in the lot.

"That fight hurt your arm," she said when they were heading along the river.

"I'll live."

"You need to rest."

He laughed. "Yeah, when we get some time to ourselves."

"Now where are we going?" she asked.

"Away from the city. I'm not sure. Maybe it's better if we don't know before we get there."

While she drove, he went through the wallets he'd taken.

After he'd counted the money, he whistled. "Five thousand dollars. That should keep us going for a while without using credit cards."

"Those guys…"

"Were working on a cash basis. No credit cards. No identification." He stuffed half the money into his pocket and put the rest into her purse. Then he took the wallets apart looking for hidden compartments. There weren't any. And no additional contact information at all.

"I guess we should have looked in their shoes."

"Huh?"

"Didn't you watch reruns of *Get Smart?* He was always hiding stuff in his shoes."

She laughed, then asked, "What if they'd been stopped by the cops?"

"Judging from their behavior when they found us, I'm guessing they would have tried to shoot their way out of it."

She winced. "What are we going to do?"

"They were after *me.* Guys from the mob. Which means I put you in danger by having you with me. I was afraid of that," he added.

She gave him a fierce look. "Do not say we should split up. If we had, they would have gotten you. And before that, George would have gotten me. We're safer together."

"I guess you knew I was thinking about…separating."

She put her hand on his knee and said the next part silently, he assumed to emphasize that they were better together than apart.

*Of course I knew! And you'd better promise me that we will stick together—no matter what.*

The depths of her feelings might have shocked him if he hadn't felt something similar. When he didn't answer at once, she clenched her hand on his knee. "Say it!"

"Okay. We will stick together."

"And we will find out how we got these mental powers. And we will strengthen them."

"Yes."

A rest stop was coming up. When she pulled into the parking area, he looked at her, then caught what was in her mind as she cut the engine and reached for him.

When he gathered her into his arms, she started to shake. He was trembling, too, as they stroked their hands over each other and kissed with a desperation and passion that made his head spin.

"I just want to be safe. With you."

"I know."

She gripped his arm. "And don't start that stuff again about my being safer without you."

"The mob…"

"Don't."

She moved her mouth against his, as if that could stop the unwanted thoughts running through his head.

They were lost to each other. Lost to the world, kissing and touching and celebrating their escape from the wise-guys—until someone rapped on the window beside her, and she jumped.

For a terrible moment Luke thought it was one of the men who had found them at Emily's apartment. But it was just a teenager grinning at them through the window.

Luke gave him a look that would have killed if they'd had that ability.

The kid's expression changed in a split second, and he hurried off. When Luke's focus shifted back to Gabriella, she fumbled for his hand and gripped it tightly.

"What is it?" he asked, trying to read her, but her thoughts weren't clear to him.

"Something…" she whispered.

"What?"

"I feel like someone was watching us."

He looked around the parking area in alarm, then relaxed. "Just that jerk who thought it was funny to interrupt us."

"No. I mean, someone else, far away who can see things… psychically."

He stared at her, fighting a feeling of dread. "You're sure?"

"Of course not. But I think someone knows we're… connected."

"Someone who wants to help us…or harm us?" he pressed.

She sighed. "I wish I knew."

"Maybe we can figure it out if we strengthen our powers. If they can spy on us, maybe we can spy on them."

"Which means we need some privacy to experiment. Are we far enough from the city to find a room?"

"I don't think so. Why don't you let me drive?"

"Your arm's okay?"

"Yeah."

She climbed out and looked around, and he knew she was still coping with the spooky feeling that a remote viewer could eavesdrop on them.

One more thing they had to worry about. But there was nothing either one of them could do about it at the moment.

When she slipped into the passenger seat and buckled her seat belt, he took off, still heading away from the city.

He drove to Bayou Monroe, a small, quiet town. First they stopped at a discount department store where they shopped separately and each paid cash for casual jeans, T-shirts and baseball caps.

They found a motel with cabins, and this time she checked in. The minute they stepped inside, she closed the door and reached for him, and he came into her arms.

They'd had no real opportunity for privacy since the men had found Luke that morning.

Finally they were alone, and the hot, frantic kisses they exchanged made his head spin.

Still, he knew this was about more than satisfying their need for each other.

Intimate contact had cemented the connection between them, and it might be the key to their survival.

His mouth moved feverishly over hers, her taste familiar and intoxicating. She returned the passion with something near desperation.

He wanted to tell her to slow down, but he couldn't say the words—or rein himself in.

His hands found the hem of the T-shirt she'd bought and slipped under, stroking across the skin of her back.

Electricity arched between them, as she strove to tell him with her mouth and body and hands how much she wanted him.

He lifted his lips a fraction, his breath rough. "We need to use this for more than...pleasure."

"I want…you."

"I want you, too. But I want more."

He felt her silent protest, but she knew he was right. They had almost gotten killed this morning. Their shared talent had saved them.

"What should we do?" she whispered.

He grinned at her. "This is working pretty well."

She let her head drop to his shoulder, clinging to him as she dragged in air.

He leaned back against the wall, taking her with him, feeling energy surging back and forth between them. In fact, he was sure he was on the verge of seeing sparks fly.

He smiled at the thought.

Striving to keep the idea in his mind from transmitting itself to her, he turned her in his arms so that her back was cradled against his front. His hands slid up and down her sides, then moved inward to capture her breasts, stoking her arousal.

He knew she felt his mind reaching for hers. More than reaching. As he stared into the room, his breath caught. He could see little crackles of mini-lightning skittering across the floor and pooling around chair and bed legs.

*Look at that.*

She gasped.

*How?*

*I thought of it, and you gave me the power. But let's switch. You make the sparks fly.*

*I'll try.*

He felt her focus on the effect, and he mentally stepped back as she increased the size of the dots of light, giving them more brightness.

"How am I doing that?" she breathed.

"You're asking me?"

"Would it hurt if that touched us?"

"I don't know."

She might be new at this, but she increased the paranormal lights, and he felt the temperature inside the room rise.

As she focused on the effect, he reached behind her and unhooked her bra, then slipped his hands under her shirt again, pushing the bra out of the way as he took her nipples between his thumbs and fingers, pulling and squeezing.

She gasped, and he knew she'd forgotten what she was supposed to be doing.

"Concentrate," he murmured.

*How can I, when you're driving me crazy?*

*Let the arousal work for us. Fuel the erotic feelings into the visual energy.*

*You've got great powers of description.*

Moments later, he saw a small shower of fairy lights flicker around a chair.

*Oh!*

He couldn't see her face, but he knew she was grinning as she moved the energy across the floor to the bed.

"Very nice," he murmured, as his hands went to the front of her jeans. He pulled open the button at the top, then lowered her zipper.

When his fingers slipped into her panties, she gasped.

*What are you doing?*

*Giving us a little power jolt.*

He held her bottom pressed to his erection as his hand slipped into the slick, wet folds of her sex while his other hand played with her breasts, teasing them as he built her passion.

He knew she was struggling to hold her focus as she climbed toward orgasm. When he felt her body shudder with release, he saw a shower of small fires exploding around the cabin.

As she came undone, the rag rug began to smolder, and she made a strangled sound.

"Not to worry." Luke eased her against the wall, then dodged around her, snatched up the rug and carried it into the bathroom, where he ran water on the fabric, preventing it from bursting into flame.

Gabriella staggered after him into the bathroom, zipping her jeans, staring at the rug.

"Is it ruined?"

"It would have been, but I caught it in time."

She goggled. "We did that?"

He grinned at her. "I guess you're pretty hot."

"Together."

"I'm not absolutely sure what I did."

"We can figure it out—together."

She reached for him. "Aside from the sparks, I think we neglected you in that exchange."

She brought his mouth to hers for a long, passionate kiss while she undid the button at the top of his jeans. After lowering the zipper, she reached inside, closing her hand around his distended flesh.

And when she sent him a vivid picture of what she intended to do, she reveled in his reaction.

EXHAUSTED FROM MAKING love and making sparks, Gabriella staggered to the bed with Luke. Together they turned back the covers and flopped down beside each other.

At first Gabriella's sleep was peaceful. Then a dream grabbed her and made her chest tighten painfully. She was in this room, alone. Luke had told her it was better if they separated. He'd promised he wouldn't leave, but now he was gone, and she felt an aching void open up inside her.

She had longed for a soul mate, and the power of the universe had granted her wish. She and Luke had found each other—against all odds. How could he walk away from that?

In the dream, she called out, heartsick at her loss. When

he didn't answer, she rushed from the cabin. The car was still out front. He must be here.

But where? She staggered into the bayou, still calling him. He must have heard because he was beside her on the bed again, slipping under the covers as he gathered her close.

"Gabriella, it's all right. Gabriella."

Her eyes blinked open, and she stared at him.

"I…thought you left."

"I promised I wouldn't."

"Where were you?"

"In the chair. Reading."

"Thank the Lord you're here." She pushed herself up and looked across the room. Apparently he'd been sitting in one of the chairs with papers spread out around him on the floor and the table.

Papers?

When she saw what they were, her mood shifted abruptly, and anger flared.

"Those are my mom's property," she said in a voice she couldn't quite hold steady.

IT WAS FOUR IN THE AFTERNOON when George looked up in surprise as an older man with salt-and-pepper hair stepped into his hospital room.

He turned to the cop in the doorway and said, "I'll take it from here."

George had never seen the newcomer before but he was pretty sure who he was.

The man closed the door and held out a shopping bag. "Here's something for you to wear. Get dressed."

"You were coming at two in the morning."

"I never like to make firm plans. Get dressed."

"How come I can leave?"

"Because you're on special assignment with the Secret Service. And I'm your boss. I have the papers to prove it."

"Oh."

"Come on. Let's split."

George didn't like the setup. And he was pretty sure the guy was wearing stuff on his face that changed his appearance.

Could he get away before the guy got him into a car?

Picking up the bag, he walked into the bathroom and closed the door as if he was modest or something. That bitch Gabriella must have gotten out the bathroom window at the motel. There was a window in this bathroom, too, but he knew he was on the third floor. Too far to jump. Was there some way to climb down without breaking his neck?

# Chapter Eleven

Luke kept his gaze on Gabriella. "You don't want me looking through your mom's papers?" he asked, hearing the edge in his voice. He was an investigative journalist. Research was his forte, and he'd thought he was doing Gabriella a favor by using his time to good advantage while she got some much-needed sleep. Apparently not.

"I..."

He watched her take her bottom lip between her teeth and hurried to explain himself. "You were sleeping. I didn't want to wake you. I thought I'd start looking through these."

"They're private. And—and, I wasn't even sure I wanted to share them."

He kept his gaze fixed on her. "Are you saying they're more private than what's in your mind?"

She stared back, and he waited with the breath shallow in his lungs to hear what she was going to say now. They'd gotten close to each other. Closer than he'd ever imagined with anyone. But neither one of them quite knew how to handle it.

"Sorry," he said in a tight voice. "I thought we were trying to figure out why we...developed psychic talents. And you risked getting kidnapped to bring these boxes along."

"Yes."

"But you didn't want me to look through the papers without your express permission?"

He saw her considering his words and his tone. "I'm sorry. I'm not used to…sharing so much. My mother was that way, too. I guess I inherited it from her."

"Okay."

"I'm on edge. What did you find?"

He wasn't willing to switch topics so quickly. "I think we'd better deal with the basics of the relationship first. You didn't want me to leave you. Are we in this together—or not?"

"Together." She swallowed. "All my life I longed to be close to someone. I saw how warm and comfortable people were with each other. I wanted that…so much. I thought I was…damaged. Abnormal. Then…I met you. And everything changed. But…it's hard to trust it. I think that's why I was dreaming that you'd left."

"I know. I'm sorry."

"And I'm so sorry that I reacted to your looking through the papers. Maybe it's because my mother never let me look at them."

"She didn't?"

"No."

He reached for her again. When she snuggled against him, some of the tension went out of him, but there was still something important he had to tell her.

"Everything you said about being alone. Feeling defective. That was true for me, too."

"And now we have more than anybody else."

"Uh-huh. But both of us are afraid to trust that it won't… vanish. So maybe we push to see if it will all blow up in our faces."

She nodded against his shoulder.

They sat together on the bed, each of them reaching out to

the other, each of them desperate to make everything right between them. Too bad there was no way to figure out the rest of their lives. Not when they were both operating under the terrible tension of being hunted.

"Now that I'm thinking clearly again, did you find out anything we can use?" she asked.

"I'm not sure, but I did come across something interesting. Did you know your mother was treated at a fertility clinic in Houma, Louisiana?"

Gabriella blinked. "No." She considered the implications. "That means she went to a lot of trouble and spent a lot of money to have a baby. Then she got me—and I wasn't what she'd longed for."

"Not your fault. We both know that."

"You think our…talent has something to do with her going to that clinic?"

He shrugged.

"But the next logical question is— Did *your* mother go there?"

Again, all he could do was shrug.

"Did she ever talk about it?"

"No."

"What was the name of the place?"

"The Solomon Clinic."

She shook her head. "That doesn't mean anything to me."

"Me, either, but it's possible that we both were conceived as the result of treatments there."

"Now that you mention it, I remember going *somewhere* for tests when I was little. But you don't remember anything like that?"

He shook his head.

"Did your family live in Louisiana?"

"New Jersey. But we moved there when I was really little.

I don't remember anything about where we came from, and they never talked much about it."

"Which could mean they didn't want you or anyone else to know."

"Maybe. But why?"

He slung his arm around her, studying the pictures in her mind, seeing her in a waiting room with parents sitting on chairs around the walls and kids in the center of the room playing.

"If your mother went there, maybe your parents thought all the tests were intrusive," she said. "Or they were upsetting you or something."

"Maybe. Or maybe my dad just found a better job on the East Coast."

"What did he do?"

"He was a science teacher."

"Are we going to Houma?" she asked.

"Yeah. But we're going to keep a very low profile. And first I'm going to do as much internet research as I can."

"I think we also need to practice our…skills."

When he gave her a wolfish grin, she went on quickly, "I mean try talking mind to mind when we're not touching. Find out how far apart we can be."

"When those guys came after me and you told me what you were going to do, I was downstairs."

"Right, but I could see you out the window. Then I was desperate."

He laughed. "That seems to help."

They showered and got dressed, then Luke went outside and walked away from the cabin, and Gabriella tried to contact him.

It worked—up to about fifteen feet. Not far enough. They needed more practice.

After going out to buy a fast-food dinner, he turned on his computer, using the motel's wireless network.

There wasn't a lot of information about the Solomon Clinic, and the more he learned, the less he liked the setup.

Gabriella came and sat beside him as he worked.

"You look upset. What have you found out?"

"That the clinic burned down about six years after it was opened. And the cause was arson."

"Someone torched it? But why?"

"I'd like to know."

"There was a nurse quoted in the paper."

"We could talk to her."

"I'd rather not."

"Because?"

"I don't want to do the obvious. And anyway, I've found out she's living in a nursing home. Maybe her memory isn't good enough."

"Then what?"

"I'm going to look up other nurses and doctors who practiced in town. See if any of them took jobs shortly after the clinic burned."

"That could take some time."

"Not as much as you think."

"Is there anything I can do?"

"See if you can turn up something else in your mom's papers."

"You don't think I'll find anything. You just think it will keep me busy."

"Sorry. It's inconvenient having someone eavesdrop on every notion that flits through my head."

"And inconvenient to have my annoyance bounce back at you."

"Yeah."

She turned away, and he went back to work.

Gabriella finished reading the papers without comment and turned on the television set in the cabin. She watched some cooking shows, and he could hear the echoes of her comments as she critiqued the chefs.

*You'd do a better job.*

*I hope so.*

When she got bored with that, she switched to a local news channel. The items were unremarkable until he heard Gabriella drag in a startled breath.

"What?"

"It's coming next," she whispered, her whole body rigid.

# *Chapter Twelve*

The announcer's voice turned grave, alerting the audience to something unpleasant.

"A patient who had been in police custody and left the Lafayette Community Hospital without being discharged was found dead in a swampy area outside of town. There was some initial confusion about his identity, but the man has been identified as George Camden. He had been shot."

"That's him," Gabriella whispered.

"You're jumping to conclusions."

She gave him a piercing look. "It's a small town. How many people named George were in police custody in the hospital?"

"We don't know that's where he was."

"Come on. Let yourself make an educated guess. You wounded him and he was in the hospital. And if it's him, it's good news for us. Because now he's not after…me."

He sensed her thoughts continuing to spin.

*However, someone murdered him.*

"Or not," he answered.

"What do you mean?"

"The news report says he was shot. He could have killed himself for all we know. If it's really him."

"We could go back to Lafayette and try to find out."

His vision turned inward as he thought about the pros and

cons of making a detour. "If we do, someone could be waiting there for us."

"Why do you think so?"

He sighed. "I'd like to feel relieved that George isn't hunting us. But we don't even know why he was after your mother—then you."

When she started to speak, he plowed ahead. "The most likely assumption is that he was working for someone who was dissatisfied with his performance."

"That's a harsh way to put it."

"George was a nasty guy. His employer could be worse."

"Why did he hire George?"

"He could be too cautious to be caught with his hands dirty."

"They why did he murder George?"

"He's getting impatient. But we're into massive speculation now."

He could feel more questions churning in her mind.

"What if it has something to do with Houma?" she asked. "I mean assuming he wasn't after me for my pecan pie recipe. What else is there?"

"We don't have enough information to make a connection to Houma."

"But we'll settle one thing if we know George is off our backs."

"You want to look at his body," he finally said, knowing what was in the back of her mind.

"Is that a bad idea?"

"I don't know."

"He was trying to kidnap me. He tried to kill you. He shot you. I want to make sure he's dead."

He felt the emotions behind her words and something else. Something she was working hard to keep hidden.

She rushed on. "And we can practice our skills."

"How exactly?"

"We talked about various things we might be able to do. What about something like…"

When she gave him a couple of examples, he grinned. She might be right. If they went to Lafayette first, they could have a dress rehearsal for Houma.

IN THE CHEAP MOTEL ROOM he'd rented, Bill Wellington examined his face in the mirror. He'd used a partial latex mask when he'd sprung George from the hospital. And he'd made sure not to touch anything where he could leave fingerprints.

He'd gotten rid of the bungler. But that left him with some unpalatable choices. He could start again with some other operative who was just as likely as George and that other guy, Carter Frederick, to screw up. Or he could take over the job himself.

If he chose the latter course, he had to proceed with extreme caution.

He knew where Dr. Douglas Solomon had been living the last time he'd checked. He'd better verify the man's whereabouts, then decide on his next move.

"SHOULDN'T WE GET GOING?" she asked, obviously anxious to try out her plan now that they'd made the decision.

"Let me find out where the morgue is. And also the layout so we aren't bumbling around like inept imposters."

He brought up a town directory and found that the morgue was at St. Stephens Hospital. From there he went to a schematic of the building, amazed at how much you could just pull off the internet.

Pointing to the screen, he said, "You go in the south entrance of the main building. Then the cold storage is straight down the hall and to the right."

"Always a good idea to look like we know where we're going," she answered, putting bravado into her voice.

They stowed the luggage and the boxes of papers in the car. Although they'd rented the cabin for two nights, they wouldn't be coming back.

First they stopped to mail the duplicates of Luke's manuscript and his research materials. Then they went to a discount department store for "business casual" attire.

Back on the road, they discussed several options.

"How ambitious is this operation?" Luke asked.

"Let's go for the easiest scenario and see if we can pull it off."

They stopped at a copy shop, where Luke used one of the computers to scan his driver's license, then substitute a different header and a different name instead of Luke Buckley.

Then he printed out the results and cut out the new ID. On brief inspection, it looked like some sort of official document, but he knew it would never hold up to scrutiny. He was praying that their mental powers would make the difference.

They arrived at the hospital complex just as it was getting dark and drove around the access road. After getting the lay of the land, they parked in the visitor's lot and walked around to the south entrance.

They'd agreed that he would do the talking, with her giving him the extra force he'd need to pull off the illusion they'd discussed. Of course, if it didn't work, they'd better be prepared to run like hell.

He knew Gabriella caught the thought.

*Just kidding.*

*You're right. We may need to leave fast. Should we have a smoke bomb ready to hide our escape?*

*I hope we won't need it.*

A guard was standing at the door.

Luke strode up to him as if he owned the place. "FBI Special Agents Simons and Mosley," he said, reaching into his pocket and pulling out his wallet, then showing the altered driver's license through the plastic window.

As he did, he sent the guard a message. *I am Special Agent Simons. That's what it says on the card. I am FBI Special Agent Simons.* Gabriella pressed her shoulder to his. He could feel her sending him energy, adding to the strength of his charade. Still he felt his heart begin to pound as he waited to find out what would happen next.

The guard looked from the card to Luke, his brow wrinkled. Luke watched the man's lips move. It had his picture and the right words, but it wasn't any kind of official government ID.

*Special Agent Simons. Special Agent Mosley.* Luke silently repeated, striving to beam the name at the guard. It was difficult to do, when he didn't know exactly what would work. But the energy he could feel flowing from Gabriella was reassuring.

His breath turned shallow as long seconds passed while the guard considered the two people standing in front of him. Luke kept his face impassive as he continued broadcasting the false information.

Finally the man nodded. "Go on in."

"Thank you."

Luke and Gabriella stepped inside and walked purposefully down the hall.

When they had turned the corner, he heard her breathe out a little sigh.

*We did it.*

*And he didn't ask why we were here.*

He squeezed her hand, then pulled his arm away, striving to look like they were professionals.

They found the refrigerated room where the bodies were stored.

Luke felt Gabriella shiver as she looked around the darkened area.

Finding the switch, he turned on a dim overhead light, then watched her zero in on the wall of stainless storage drawers.

As a reporter, he'd been in places like this before. He knew from her thoughts that she'd only witnessed similar scenes in the movies.

The room was cold, and there was a faint odor that made both of them take shallow breaths.

"Are you okay?" he whispered.

"Yes."

She might have reached for his hand. Instead, she wrapped her arms around her shoulders and rubbed her palms up and down her arms.

Luke gave her a concerned look. He'd caught some of her thoughts, but he knew that she was blocking some of what was in her mind.

"What is it?"

"This place spooks me."

"Yeah. Let's do it and split," he said as he walked to the wall and started reading the labels. There were three dead bodies in here. When he found the right storage compartment, he pulled it open.

Gabriella hung back for a few seconds. Then, with teeth gritted, she hurried forward and looked into the drawer.

Her indrawn breath had him pulling her close.

"It's him all right," he growled. "And he's got a bullet hole in the middle of his forehead."

She stared down at the man who had tried to kidnap her, a look of distaste on her face. "He was a scumbag. He could have gotten shot trying to rob a gas station," she whispered.

"Then why would he end up dumped in the swamp?"

She made a strangled sound. "I was just trying to put…a spin on it."

"Like I said before, I think we have to assume he was working for someone who got frustrated with his failures."

"You mean to grab me."

Luke nodded. "We confirmed he was murdered. Let's get out of here."

He knew she wanted to leave, but she stood where she was, indecision whirling in her brain.

"Gabriella?"

A split second before she moved, he caught her intent and tried to snatch her away from the storage drawer. But he was already too late. She reached out and put her hand on the man's cold shoulder.

He watched in horror as her eyes fluttered closed and her knees buckled.

Before she hit the tile floor, he caught her, his curse filling the little room.

"Gabriella? Gabriella? What is it? What happened?"

She didn't move, didn't speak. When he tried to reach her thoughts, it was as if a solid barrier had dropped into place, separating her mind from his.

As he cradled her against his chest, a primal fear he had never known clawed at him. He was still calling her name, but nothing changed. She was completely unresponsive, and he had to get her out of here. But where were they going?

Not to the car. He'd have to drive somewhere, and he knew she needed him *now.*

Desperately, he tried to remember the schematic of the morgue. He'd been interested in getting to this room, then leaving the same way they'd come in. But he remembered that there was a back entrance into the hospital. Should he take her out that way?

Or was there some place in here where he could lay her down?

He gritted his teeth, hating not knowing which way to go. Finally, he turned to his side and pushed the drawer closed with his shoulder, then carried Gabriella into the hallway.

The guard would still be at the front door, which meant he couldn't leave that way carrying "Agent Mosley." Instead, he turned in the other direction and found the door that led into the hospital basement.

Above it was a sign that said "No return entry."

If they went out, they weren't coming back this way.

Making a snap decision, he pushed on the bar that opened the door, then stepped through into a dimly lit corridor with steam pipes along the ceiling.

What if he met somebody? How would he explain that he was carrying an unconscious woman?

No sooner had the thought popped into his mind than he heard footsteps coming in the other direction. He rushed forward to the next door he found along the corridor. To his vast relief, when he turned the knob, it opened.

He stepped inside, probably just in time, and breathed out a small sigh as he heard whoever it was walk past. He felt along the wall and found a row of switches.

When he flipped one on, dim light came from an overhead fixture. They were in a large storage area with supplies on shelves that were laid out in rows with narrow aisles. He made his way through them until he came to an area where he couldn't be seen from the door. Then he grabbed some packages of blankets. Still holding Gabriella, he awkwardly spread out several blankets. After lowering her to the makeshift bed, he eased down beside her.

Her color was good and her breathing was even, but she showed no signs of waking up.

"Gabriella," he murmured. "Come back to me."

When she didn't stir, fear gripped him. Over the past few days, he'd forged a connection with her that he'd never expected to find with anyone in this life or the next. Now he understood on a deep, gut-wrenching level that he might lose her.

The idea was so terrible that he tried to shove it away, but it hovered at the edge of his thoughts.

Leaning back against a shelf, he picked her up in his arms and cradled her in his lap, hugging her to him. He wanted to yell at her. He wanted to raise his voice and tell her she'd been a fool to touch that dead thug.

But what good would that do? It was over and done, and he had to deal with what had happened.

He struggled to calm his roiling emotions. There was no point in blaming her. His only option was to bring her back. Because the alternative had become unthinkable.

He closed his mind to everything around him, shutting out the world as he hugged her to him, unconsciously rocking her in his arms as he focused only on her.

*I can't lose you. Not now. Come back to me,* he pleaded. *Just come back. If you don't, I'll die.*

# Chapter Thirteen

From far away, Luke thought he felt something stirring in Gabriella's mind, and his heart leaped. She'd been in some place where he couldn't reach her. Now it was as if a crack had opened up in the wall between them. Just a small chink, but he could shout through it and know his words were penetrating.

*Gabriella? What happened? Where are you?*

She didn't answer, but pictures flashed in his mind. They were blurry, but he thought they might be the man's memories. Somehow Gabriella had picked them up.

*You saw what happened to him?*

Again, she didn't answer, but the images continued. George was riding in a car. Lying in the backseat, his hands and feet tied. The car stopped in a swampy area. A man Luke didn't recognize hauled George out and dragged him toward the swamp.

*Do you know him?* Luke asked urgently.

Again, there was no answer, and all Luke could do was keep watching the video roll.

The new guy looked to be in his sixties, with a thick head of salt-and-pepper hair, piercing hazel eyes, wide lips and a determined expression that made Luke's stomach knot. After seating his captive on a fallen log, he pulled a gun and pointed it toward George, who was now talking rapidly.

Luke couldn't hear what he was saying, but he appeared to be pleading.

The man responded.

George spoke again.

The conversation ended abruptly when the man with the gun pulled the trigger.

He felt Gabriella's body jump. Felt her shock. Her terror. Her pain.

And at the same time, she was silently calling out to Luke.

"I'm here. You're with me. You're going to be okay," he said, praying that it was true. "Wake up. You saw what happened to him. You can wake up now."

For long moments, nothing changed, and he held her with his heart pounding and his breath like fire in his chest.

Then she moaned and began to writhe in his arms. All he could do was cradle her against himself, soothe her, because he knew that the next part was worse.

He saw darkness, felt George's abject terror. The man was dead. But his mind was still working, and he was seeing a long, endless horrible future stretching in front of him.

And Gabriella was too close to that vision. It was sucking her in.

"It's not you. It's him," Luke said, struggling not to shout as he fought his own fear and desperation. "Don't go there with him. You're seeing his punishment for the immoral life he's led."

He knew she heard his words. Still, he felt her sway in the balance, her mind trying to come back to earth yet attached to the man whose death she had experienced.

"Gabriella! Stay with me."

When she didn't answer, he felt despair welling inside him.

*It's not you. It's him.*

*Is it?*

*Yes!*

*But it feels so...bad.*

He knew he must make her understand how much he needed her. With no other option, he gathered her close and lowered his mouth to hers, kissing her with a desperation that bordered on madness.

For long moments, nothing happened, and his desperation grew.

Then, finally, she began to kiss him back, and he felt tears sting his eyes.

*Thank the Lord. You're back.*

*Yes. Oh, yes. Luke!*

He raised his head and saw her eyes blink open. She looked around, trying to figure out where she was.

"In the hospital. A storage room. I carried you here after you touched George."

She clutched his arms, pressing herself against him. "I shouldn't have done it."

He couldn't stop himself from saying, "I think you almost died."

She nodded against his chest. "I'm sorry."

"I think you had to do it. I mean, you would have always wondered if you could get information from him."

Again she nodded.

"How do you get into a dead man's memories?"

She shook her head. "I don't know. But I was thinking about trying it."

"I knew you were thinking about *something* you didn't want to share with me."

"Yes."

"How did you keep me from knowing?"

"I don't know. I just tried to avoid letting it stay in my mind for long. You know, like when you're trying to remember a name, so you focus on everything else and it finally comes to you."

"Well, you fooled me. You kept me from finding out about it. I guess that's something else we need to practice. But we're getting off the subject. How did you know you'd get into his mind?"

Her mouth twisted. "I didn't. Not really. But the idea kept growing. When I saw him, I had to try it. And I did find out some things. We know that other man shot him."

"George and the other guy were talking. I couldn't hear anything."

"I could."

"Do you know the other guy's name?"

"George called him the Badger."

He made a low sound. "I don't think we can look that up on Google."

Gabriella reached for his hand and knit her fingers with his. "Before he died, George was trying to keep the guy talking. He was thinking he might get away, but it didn't work out like he hoped."

"Yeah."

"He asked the guy's real name, and the Badger told him. I guess because he figured George wasn't going to share the information with anyone. It's Bill Wellington."

"Bill Wellington," Luke repeated.

"Does that mean anything to you?"

He turned the name over in his mind. "Not yet. But now there's something we can look up, although it may not be his real name, only the one he's using now."

"Terrific."

She kept her hand on his arm. "They talked a little, before Wellington pulled the trigger. I guess this really is wrapped up with that clinic in Houma. He told George that a crackpot named Dr. Douglas Solomon had been running illegal experiments."

Luke swore. "What kind of illegal experiments?"

"All Wellington would say was that they hadn't turned out the way Dr. Solomon expected."

Gabriella lifted her head toward Luke, her eyes bleak. "So I could be some kind of freak. Well, that's what I always thought. Now I've got confirmation."

"Stop it! You don't even know if the Wellington guy was telling the truth."

"I think he was—from his point of view."

Luke thought about that. "Maybe we should assume he was after you because he was trying to get more information about the children from the clinic."

She nodded.

"We need to go to Houma."

"Later. First we need to go somewhere you can relax and recover from your trip into George's last memories. But we can't go back the way we came," he added.

"Why not? You think the guard will realize we're not FBI agents?"

"Maybe we could have, but the door to the morgue locked behind us when I brought you here. I guess it works that way to keep hospital staff out. We're going to have to walk through the hospital."

"Okay."

He helped her up.

When she stood swaying on her feet, he steadied her. Just as they started toward the door, it pushed inward, and Luke froze at the sound of someone entering the room where they'd taken shelter.

# *Chapter Fourteen*

Luke felt Gabriella shudder. She was in no shape to confront anyone. For that matter, neither was he.

*Could we hide in here?* she asked.

*Don't know.*

The option was taken away from them when a man stepped around the corner and gave them a startled look. He was in his thirties, with sandy hair and a spray of freckles across his nose. He was pushing a supply cart. Probably a stock clerk. His name tag read Calvin Jerrold.

His gaze fixed on them. "What are you doing here?"

"I am Dr. Simons, and this is Dr. Mosley," Luke said, using the same names as before and gesturing toward Gabriella.

Jerrold's eyes narrowed. "I don't think so. I think you're stealing hospital supplies."

"No," Luke answered, still madly projecting the names he'd just given.

But it wasn't doing any good. He felt Gabriella trying to feed him energy, but after her ordeal with George Camden, she simply couldn't muster the power she'd had before.

The guy took a step back and reached for the cell phone on his belt.

Now what? Assault an innocent bystander? The thought twisted Luke's guts, but it might be the only choice.

Even as the desperate thought flashed through his mind, he was still projecting toward Jerrold, trying to get the message through. And finally, he felt Gabriella muster some psychic energy.

It was as if someone was pressing down on a contact point. Moments later, the pressure became steadier, but was it enough to accomplish anything?

*I am Dr. Simons. Dr. Simons. I have every right to be here. Dr. Mosley and I are just leaving.*

Luke kept his gaze on the hand hovering over the phone.

*Let me.* Gabriella raised her large, appealing eyes toward Calvin Jerrold.

"We were just leaving," she said in a warm voice. "We were here on an inspection trip from Monumental Insurance. We haven't taken anything, and we will give you an excellent report. You're just the type of employee this hospital needs."

Jerrold stared at her. "I am?"

"Yes. Very alert and on your toes. Quick to take responsibility, but I know you have work to do, and we'll get out of your way," she said.

Luke kept projecting the information he'd given the guy.

*I am Dr. Simons. Dr. Simons. I have every right to be here. Dr. Mosley and I are just leaving.*

When the man nodded, Luke let out the breath he'd been holding.

They walked around him and out of the supply room. Once in the hall, Luke dared to hope that they'd escaped. He wanted to start running, but Gabriella gripped his arm, slowing him down.

It turned out he'd been right all along. When they were almost to the elevator, Jerrold charged out of the supply closet.

"Stop." His voice boomed behind them.

Praying that Jerrold hadn't taken the time to call for help,

Luke rushed back and grabbed the phone, hurling it to the floor. Before he could change his mind, he slammed the guy against the wall, and all the fight went out of him.

As Jerrold made a moaning sound and slipped to the floor, Gabriella gasped.

"It's going to be okay," Luke answered, praying he wasn't lying.

Teeth clenched, he dragged the limp man back into the closet. He hated to tie him up, but he didn't see any alternative. He found packages of IV cord, which he used to tie the guy's hands. Finally, he used a pair of scrub pants for a gag.

When he looked up, Gabriella was staring at him, wide-eyed.

"Don't hurt him."

"I don't want to."

Jerrold blinked and focused on her, making a pleading sound.

"We don't want to hurt you," she said in a soothing voice. She looked at Luke. *Help me.*

He nodded.

She focused on the supply clerk again. *Dr. Simons is blond and about six foot four. That's how he overpowered you. He's so big. And Dr. Mosley is tall, too. She's got strawberry-colored hair. And green eyes.*

In his mind, Luke listened to her repeat the description several times.

"Somebody will find you soon," he said, hoping it was true. Maybe they could call the hospital when they were far enough away.

"He was just doing his job," Gabriella murmured as they stepped into the hall again and walked past the elevator to the stairs.

"I know. I'm sorry. We tried to con him, but neither one of us has enough juice to do it now."

They reached the main floor and started toward the lobby. At least there weren't many people around. Still, it was the longest walk Luke had ever taken.

When they were finally out of the building, he gulped in a breath of the humid night air.

"Thank the Lord," Gabriella whispered.

He kept his arm around her, helping her to the car and opening the door. As she collapsed into the passenger seat, he came around to the other side and slipped behind the wheel.

There was so much he wanted to say, but he had to get away before Jerrold got loose.

"Do you think the description will hold up?" he asked as he headed for the exit.

"I don't know. I hope so. And Simons and Mosley are the only names he's got. If he compares notes with the guard up front, they're not going to agree." He swung his gaze toward her. "I'd better ask. He's not someone you ever met in town, right?"

"Right," she said in a weary voice.

As he drove out of town, he saw she was sitting with her eyes closed, and he knew she was at the end of her strength. When she dozed off, he wanted to let her sleep.

Before he had gotten a few miles from the hospital, a police car with flashing lights came speeding down the highway, directly toward them.

# Chapter Fifteen

Luke was just passing a swampy area thick with the hulking trees, a lot like the place where they'd gotten stuck on the plantation—a thousand years ago. Spotting a narrow road, he turned off, cutting the lights and driving into the shadows of the trees, praying that the cops hadn't spotted him.

He wondered what the hell they were going to do if the officers came to them. Not shoot their way out.

*Drive on past,* he broadcast several times, wondering if it was doing any good.

For whatever reason, the police car continued toward the hospital.

"Now what?" Gabriella whispered.

"I'm thinking." And not liking his alternatives. He'd wanted to stop at a motel in the next town. That was out of the question now. Desperation was forcing a different decision.

He backed up cautiously onto the road, then kept driving toward town. When he began seeing widely spaced driveways, he slowed, looking for a house with no lights on. And, ideally, a pile of newspapers that hadn't been delivered.

Finally spotting what he wanted, he turned in at a gravel lane and drove toward a one-story dwelling surrounded by a grove of trees.

"What are we doing?" Gabriella asked.

"Finding a place to stay."

"What do you mean? This is somebody's house."

"Yeah." He pulled to a stop near the front door. "Wait here while I investigate."

"No."

"It would be better if we don't both get shot."

She winced but stayed in the car as he got out and stood for a moment, sniffing the air for cooking smells, listening for a barking dog.

The property seemed deserted. After he rang the bell at the front door, got no answer and didn't hear a dog barking, he went around the back and looked for an alarm system. As far as he could tell, there was none, so he began trying windows.

The second one had a weak lock, and he was able to push it up and climb inside. When nobody appeared with a gun, he opened the back door.

Outside, he walked quietly around to the car. Gabriella jumped as he opened the driver's door.

"Are we leaving?" she asked, her voice sounding so hopeful that he wished he could give her the answer she wanted. But they had passed the point where law-abiding behavior would to do them any good.

"We're parking around back."

"Oh, goody." She turned to look at him. "We started out perfectly innocent. Now…we've left my friend's apartment in a mess, assaulted a man and broken into someone's house."

"We won't steal anything—well, except maybe some food."

"Super."

Still, she followed him inside, through the kitchen and into a darkened family room. Moonlight filtered in through a window, giving them enough illumination to see the layout but not enough to pick up a lot of personal details. Which was good. The less they knew about these people, the better.

After looking around for several moments, she plopped down on a high-backed sofa.

He came over and sat beside her.

When she said nothing, he reached for her hand. He'd never been great at discussing his feelings, but there was something he needed to say.

"Back at the hospital when you went unconscious…." He dragged in a breath and started again. "I was scared spitless. I was afraid I'd lose you. I love you. I need you. If anything had happened to you, I don't know what I would have done."

"Oh, Luke. Luke." She had been sitting stone-still. Now she turned toward him, pulling him into her arms, and they clung together.

"I love you," she answered him. "I was afraid of how much I need you."

They held on to each other, each glad that they had said the words.

"We're in bad trouble," she whispered.

"We'll fix it."

"We don't know what we're going to find in Houma," she added. "Remember what Wellington said to George about that clinic doing freak experiments."

Luke felt his anger rising. "Don't put any stock in what that jerk said."

"He was talking to a man he was going to kill."

"All the more reason to discount it," he argued, even when he couldn't stop his own doubts.

"We should sleep while we can."

"Then what?"

"Let's wait until we're feeling fresher."

They curled together on the sofa, comforted by the closeness. He had the vague idea that he should keep guard, but he also knew that he couldn't keep going with no sleep.

He awoke before dawn, feeling steadier. When he shifted to get off the couch, Gabriella grabbed his arm. "Where are you going?"

"To shower."

She sat up and ran her hand through her hair. "Is it okay to use the shower?"

"We'll be neat."

She sighed, and he knew she didn't want to use anything in the house, but that desire was outweighed by her craving to get clean.

He used the bathroom first, then got out of her way. While she was getting ready, he hit a bit of luck when he checked the garage. With the household equipment, he found electrical tape, which he used to change the "I" on his license plate to an "L", hoping it would throw the cops off if they'd been caught on surveillance cameras in the hospital parking lot.

When he came back, he stopped short and stared at Gabriella. Apparently she'd given up keeping her hands off the owner's property. She'd used scissors to give herself a pixie cut. It was cute but startling.

"It'll grow back," she said as she held up a plastic bag. "We'll take the hair with us and get rid of it in a dumpster. And I put the towels we used in the hamper. There were others in there. Maybe they won't know we were here."

"Yeah," he agreed, wondering if the homeowners would make a police report. They wiped off everything they had touched.

After only seven hours in the borrowed house they left, heading toward Houma and staying well within the speed limit. With Luke's baseball cap firmly on his head.

The first time they saw a cop car, they both tensed, but the cruiser passed them by with only a cursory glance.

"He could check that license plate," Gabriella fretted.

"He'd have to hook into the New Jersey system, and he's got better things to do. When they actually investigate, they'll find out we didn't steal anything from the hospital or the morgue. Really, it's no big deal."

"Except the assault."

"You can bake the guy a special dessert when this is over."

She snorted.

THEY BOUGHT COFFEE AND breakfast sandwiches at a fast-food restaurant drive-through and ate in the parking lot.

"We don't have a strategy," she said as she sat staring out the front window, sipping the coffee.

"Maybe we do have to start with that nurse after all," he said. "The one who was mentioned in the article."

"And ask her questions about the clinic?"

He shook his head. "No. I'm hoping you can use your technique. If you touch her, maybe you can get the names of other people who worked there."

"And if I can't?"

"We'll come up with plan B."

GABRIELLA'S STOMACH WAS in knots. The closer they got to Houma, the more she wanted to scream at Luke to turn around and go somewhere else. Anywhere else. What if the two of them just kept driving?

"That Bill Wellington guy would still be looking for us. We couldn't go back to our lives."

"You could. He's looking for me."

"I'm not leaving you. It's going to be okay," he murmured as they crossed the town limits.

"You can say that, but you know I have the feeling something bad is going to happen here."

"What?"

"That's the worst part. I don't know."

"You have a better suggestion?"

She clenched and unclenched her hands. "I wish I did. Let's just get it over with."

They drove to the address he'd found, which turned out to be a one-story red brick residence and nursing facility for the elderly.

"I hope this works," Gabriella said as they pulled into the parking lot and Luke cut the engine.

"Do you want to leave?"

"No," she lied, then switched away from her own doubts while she focused on the building and grounds.

"It's well maintained," she murmured as they followed a winding path through well-tended gardens.

Just beyond, the double doors led to a reception area where a young woman sat at an antique desk.

Her name tag identified her as Sarah Dalton.

"Can I help you?" she asked in a gracious southern accent.

"We'd like to visit with Maven Bolton."

She tipped her head to one side. "Maven has gotten very popular."

"Oh?" Luke asked.

"Why, yes. Another couple was here to see her a couple of weeks ago."

Gabriella tensed. "Two men?"

"No, a man and a woman. About your ages," she added as she looked them up and down.

Gabriella took that in. "We…we're old friends."

"They were as well."

*That sounds weird. Should we leave?* Gabriella silently asked Luke.

*No.*

*But who were they?*

*Maybe we'll find out.*

"I'm sure she'll be pleased to see you," Ms. Dalton said, standing up and checking her watch. "Maven should be in the dayroom now."

They followed the woman down a hallway to a pleasantly large recreation room with windows looking out onto the gardens.

About twenty elderly women and a few elderly men were sitting around the room. Some were in wheelchairs. Others were in easy chairs watching television or at tables playing cards or working puzzles.

Ms. Dalton led them to a woman who was sitting by the window with a magazine in her lap. She had short gray hair and a wrinkled face, and she was wearing a nice-looking flowered blouse and tan slacks.

"Some people to see you, Maven."

The older woman looked up a bit apprehensively.

"We just stopped in to say hello," Luke said. They both pulled up chairs and sat down.

After a few moments the attendant left them.

"Are you like that other couple?" the old woman asked.

"I don't know. What can you tell us about them?" Gabriella asked, pulling her chair a little closer.

"They were getting married. They wanted to check...I don't remember if it was his or her background."

"Why?" she murmured.

Maven lowered her voice. "His...or her...mother had the fertility treatments from Dr. Solomon."

"Um," Luke answered.

"Yes. But he doesn't like me to talk about that. Not since everything came to an end."

"We won't tell anyone." Gabriella gently put her hand over the old woman's arm. For a moment, she hesitated, remembering what had happened when she'd gotten into George's mind after his death, but this had to be different. This was an elderly woman who had lived a much more conventional life. Still, she fought not to tense as she reached for Mrs. Bolton's mind. It was vague about recent events, but a rich wealth of memories flooded into Gabriella.

Luke and the old woman's voice buzzed in the background, as he pretended that he'd just come there to chat, distracting the old woman from their real mission.

Gabriella let the spoken words flow over her as she rummaged for the real information.

"You grew up here in Houma?" Luke asked.

"Uh-huh."

"Was it a good place to live?"

"I loved it here."

"And you were married?"

"Yes, but my husband died years ago."

"I'm sorry."

"I got by on my own."

"You didn't have any children?"

"We had a little boy who died."

"I'm so sorry," he said again.

The questions went on in that vein for several minutes.

*We should go,* Gabriella said silently.

*Okay.* Luke turned his attention back to the old woman. "It was nice talking to you."

"Do you know that other couple?" Mrs. Bolton asked.

"I don't think so."

"If you see them, say hello for me."

"We will," Luke replied before they turned and headed back the way they'd come. They didn't speak until they'd left the building and gotten into the car.

"That was strange," he said. "Someone else was here. Asking about the clinic."

She shuddered. "Someone else looking for us?"

"There's another explanation. What if it was someone else *like* us, doing the same thing we were?"

"If they were here, what happened to them?"

Luke shook his head, but she caught his thought.

*Let's hope they're not dead.*

*Could George have been after them?*

*I wish I knew.*

They sat for a few moments in silence, unable to come to any conclusions. Finally they turned back to the reason for coming to the nursing home.

"Did you get some names of people who worked at the clinic from her?" Luke asked.

She was glad to change the subject. "Yes."

Reaching for his hand, she let the information she'd obtained flow from her mind to his. There were two other nurses who had worked at the clinic who were also still in town.

"Now we just have to decide which one of them is our best bet." He looked at her. "Do you have any psychic insights?"

"I think Violet Goodell was the doctor's most trusted assistant."

"Why do you think so?"

"She was just out of nursing school when she took a job with him. I think she worshipped him."

"Why?"

"She thought he was brilliant. She was willing to work overtime when the rest of the staff went home."

"Which might mean she wouldn't want to talk about him." Luke pursed his lips. "But we won't know unless we ask her. Is she married?"

"If she is, she kept her professional name."

They headed for the neighborhood on the outskirts of town where Ms. Goodell lived.

Up a long driveway in an area screened off by trees and shrubs set a brick colonial with a wide portico in front. Everything was well tended.

"Very elegant," Luke said as he pulled into a parking area.

"She's got a garage and room for another couple of cars outside," he said as he cut the engine. "This place is big enough to be a bed-and-breakfast."

"Maybe she likes to impress the ladies' bridge club when she has them over."

"Maybe. But the house is certainly on the high end of Houma residences."

*Should I do the talking this time?* Gabriella asked.

*That makes sense.*

Luke squeezed her hand, feeling her tension. "Nothing bad happened back at the nursing home. Maybe our luck will hold."

"I hope so."

He climbed out and led the way to the portico.

A few moments after they'd rung the doorbell, a woman in a peach-colored sweater set came to the door. She looked to be in her late fifties, well kept and pampered, with clear brown eyes and soft blond hair done in an expensively casual style.

"Ms. Goodell?" Gabriella asked.

She eyed them with interest. "Why, yes. May I help you?"

"I hope so. Can we come in?"

"What is this about?"

Beside him, Gabriella dragged in a breath and let it out. This was it. "We'd like to talk to you about the Solomon Clinic."

Her brown eyes widened. "The Solomon Clinic? Goodness. Why, I haven't worked there in years. It burned down, you know."

"Yes, we do know. Can we come in?"

"I suppose so. But there's not much I can tell you. What is your interest in the clinic?"

Gabriella couldn't quite hold her voice steady. "I believe I was conceived as the result of treatments Dr. Solomon gave my mother."

"Interesting. What is your name, dear?"

"Gabriella Boudreaux."

The woman smiled. "Oh, yes, your mother was Marian, and I do remember you. Our children used to come back to the clinic for physical exams."

"You remember me?" Gabriella asked.

"Of course. You were such a sweet girl." She led the way to a formal living room done in pastels.

"You make yourselves comfortable," she said. "I'll just go and get you some homemade cookies and lemonade."

"No need," Luke said quickly.

"Oh, it's no trouble at all for one of the doctor's children. I'll be right back."

After she hurried out of the room, Luke and Gabriella exchanged glances.

*Does that reception seem a bit off?* Luke asked.

*Yes.*

*I wonder if she left to call Dr. Solomon.*

*But he's dead. Or dropped out of sight.*

Luke shrugged. *She might know where he is.*

"Maybe I ought to offer to help her in the kitchen," Gabriella murmured.

"I'll go with you."

They both stood and had started toward the hall when the front door opened. Luke stopped in his tracks as two men stepped into view.

It was the two mobsters who had caught up with him outside the New Orleans apartment, then marched him inside to kill him and Gabriella.

They were both holding guns, and they looked mad as hell.

# *Chapter Sixteen*

Gabriella stared at the two men in horror.

The bald one gave her a triumphant grin. "You thought you gave us the slip."

"How…how did you find us?" she managed to say, hoping to play for time.

"We went back to that cottage at the plantation. Turns out some of your mom's papers got caught under the chair. We came to Houma looking for you—and saw you driving around."

The guy's voice was low and controlled. But underneath the words she could hear the anger simmering. In New Orleans, she'd gotten the better of him and his buddy, and he didn't like that. Now he was planning to get even with her.

Beside her, Luke's body coiled.

"Don't try anything funny," the other one warned. "Or we'll shoot your girlfriend first. We're all getting out of here. Now," the bald man continued, "before that nice old lady comes back and gets hurt."

"Let Gabriella go," Luke said. "Your beef is with me, not her."

"She got herself into it by getting mixed up with you. Come on, both of you."

*What are we going to do?* Gabriella asked, her silent voice filled with desperation.

*You lend me energy. I'll try getting them to shoot each other.*

*Can you?*

*You have a better suggestion?*

Gabriella gritted her teeth, and he could feel energy pouring into him. He knew getting the thugs to focus on each other wasn't going to be easy. But they had no alternative.

*Point your guns at each other and shoot,* he ordered, then silently chanted the instruction over and over.

The two men, once united in their purpose, grew confused. "What the hell are you doing?" the bald one growled.

"Nothing,"

"You're lying. Stop it."

When the thug held firm, Luke knew the technique had backfired. It looked as if they weren't going to wait to drag him out of here before they shot him.

He could feel Gabriella desperately trying to boost his mental energy, but these men had apparently developed some kind of tolerance for his extrasensory abilities.

His only alternative was to press on. But at that moment a flutter of movement at the door made both men turn.

Ms. Goodell stepped into the room. She was holding a plate of cookies in one hand. The other was covered by a dish towel. "My goodness," she gasped. "What's this?"

One of the wiseguys cursed. Then came a hissing sound as a projectile whizzed from under the dish towel and hit the bald mobster.

A look of perplexity crossed his features, and he tried to aim his gun at the older woman, but somehow he couldn't manage to change the direction of his hand.

As the bald mobster's knees buckled, a white-haired man stepped in the front door. He was holding a strange little gun, which he fired at the other intruder—who joined his friend on the floor.

The newcomer gave Gabriella and Luke a quizzical look. They both stared back at him.

"Are you Dr. Solomon?" Gabriella breathed.

"Yes."

"But I thought…you were dead."

He chuckled. "If so, the reports of my death have been greatly exaggerated."

"But you kept a low profile."

"Yes."

"Where did you come from?"

"As it happens, I was visiting Violet when you arrived." He looked at the thugs on the floor. "When I saw these two rough-looking men arrive, I was pretty sure they were up to no good. Who are they?"

"New Jersey mobsters. Sorry I brought trouble to you."

"No harm done. They'll be out cold for hours, but I believe we should get them into custody."

"You mean call the police?"

"Yes. Of course. But for now my private security force will see that they don't cause any more trouble."

"Why do you need security?" Luke asked.

"Like you, I have enemies." He gestured with his hand toward the back of the house. "Why don't we go out on the porch where we can be comfortable?"

Luke made no move to follow as he studied the doctor. The famous Douglas Solomon. Was he a crackpot as Bill Wellington had said? Or was he a dangerous genius?

Luke kept his gaze on the doctor. "I'd like to know why you've been in hiding all these years."

"If you want specifics—because a man who now calls himself Bill Wellington has been hunting me."

"Bill Wellington?" Gabriella dragged in a startled breath.

"You've heard that name?" the doctor asked, his tone sharpening.

"Yes." She glanced at Luke, then back at the doctor. "He sent a thug named George Camden to kidnap me."

"It looks like you two have had a pretty rough time," Dr. Solomon said sympathetically. Then his face hardened. "Wellington's bad news. Once he gets an idea in his head, he won't leave it alone."

"Who is he?"

"He used to have hush-hush government connections." He sighed. "Back when I was desperate to put my ideas into practice, I learned that he was giving out government research grants through the Howell Institute. I went to him for funding, which turned out to be a big mistake." He looked back at the two men. "You're sure these men don't work for Wellington, too?"

Luke sighed. "They mentioned their mob boss."

Solomon nodded. "We should get comfortable. Why don't we sit down and talk. I think we have a lot of information to exchange."

*Can we trust him?* Gabriella asked.

Luke hesitated. *No. But I don't think we can just walk out—not after what he did to the mobsters. I think we need to play along and find out what he's up to,* he answered, wishing he were doing it alone.

*Forget that.*

The two of them followed Solomon and Goodell through the dining room and onto a spacious screened porch. Luke and Gabriella sat together on a love seat where they could keep their power concentrated together if they needed it. The doctor took a comfortable wicker chair.

"Excuse me for a minute," Ms. Goodell said. "I'll go and get that lemonade."

"Please don't bother," Gabriella answered.

"No bother at all. I think we all need some refreshments."

When she returned from the kitchen, she was carrying

a tray with the pitcher of lemonade and four glasses, which she set on a wicker buffet at the side of the room.

After pouring everyone a glass, she took a wicker chair opposite the doctor.

"Please, I'm sure you're parched after that little rumpus in the hall," she said, lifting a glass to her lips.

Gabriella and Luke each took a few sips.

The doctor smiled at Gabriella. "I already know your name. Gabriella Boudreaux." He looked at Luke. "And you are?"

He hesitated for a moment then said, "Liam Bridges."

"Liam Bridges!" The doctor's face lit up as he exclaimed. "Young man, you're on a very short list."

"What kind of list?" Luke asked, instantly wary.

"We had an agreement with the women who came to us for fertility treatments. After they delivered, they were supposed to bring their children back to us for testing."

"Testing for what?"

"As you may have gathered, the main purpose of the clinic was not fertility research. We were running a program designed to create super-intelligent children."

Luke's reporter's instincts began to tingle. It sounded as if the doctor had been less than truthful with his patients.

"Did you get the results you wanted?" he asked with an edge in his voice.

"The children had a normal intelligence distribution. Which was why Wellington withdrew the funding and had the clinic burned down."

"That's a pretty extreme response."

"He's an extreme kind of guy. Well, one of his operatives did it. Yes. I said he was ruthless."

Luke wanted to hear more about that, but it seemed the doctor wasn't planning to elaborate at the moment. He kept his gaze on Luke. "Let's get back to you. Your mother was one of the few patients who broke her contract. She moved out of the area, taking you with her."

Luke stared at the man, trying to work his way through the implications. "You're saying I was a product of the clinic?"

"Yes."

"So both of us…" Gabriella's voice trailed off.

"Do you know a couple named Rachel Gregory and Jake Harper?" Solomon asked.

Gabriella's brow wrinkled. "Not personally. Doesn't Jake Harper own a restaurant in New Orleans? And other businesses?"

"Yes, but he's been in hiding recently."

"Why?" Luke asked. He was beginning to feel a little sick, probably from the strain of the past few days.

"Wellington was after him and Ms. Gregory. They're also products of the clinic."

Luke nodded. His mind had started to turn fuzzy, and he could feel his face flushing. If it hadn't been impolite, he would have asked to lie down.

He blinked, trying to clear his vision.

*I don't feel so well.* He heard the words in his mind and turned toward Gabriella. Her face looked as hot as he felt, and suddenly he knew that it wasn't from the bullet wound or the strain.

"What did…you…do to us?" he asked, struggling to get the words out.

"It was for your own protection," the doctor murmured.

"Why?" Luke gasped.

"Something's going on with Wellington. Apparently he's desperate to get his hands on some of the clinic's children. I gather he suspects you may have some unusual mental abilities."

Luke's mouth was so dry he could barely speak. "No," he denied.

The doctor's voice warmed. "All these years, I thought I failed. But I didn't, did I?"

Luke grabbed Gabriella's hand. They had to get out of here before…

He didn't know what. But when he pushed himself to a standing position, he wavered on his feet, then toppled over, dragging Gabriella down with him.

The doctor crouched over him. "You'll feel better in a while," he said. "Let's get you comfortable."

Luke struggled to focus on Dr. Solomon but his vision was too blurred. Finally it went black.

FIFTY MILES AWAY, Rachel gasped. *I felt them again. They're in bad trouble.*

*The other couple?*

*Yes. I think...I think Dr. Solomon's got them.*

Jake dragged in a startled breath.

"Solomon? You're saying he's alive after all?"

"I think so. And I think he's going to experiment on the man and woman. Luke and Gabriella. Those are their names." She paused. "That may not be *his* real name."

"Where are they?"

She made a low sound. "I don't know. But I think they were trying to find out about the Solomon Clinic."

Jake's eyes narrowed. "Do you think Solomon is still hanging around Houma?"

"That's the place to start."

He gestured toward his computer. "We've got the names of other nurses who worked at the clinic. We can ask them some questions."

Rachel swallowed. "I don't think so."

"Why not?"

"First—the obvious reason. The Badger could be watching the place. Then there's..." She stopped and started again. "Wait a minute. Maybe we do know he's in Houma. I saw a flash. Luke and Gabriella. Solomon and one of his nurses. She's still working with him."

"Doing what?"

"Knowing him, probably some kind of unsavory research."

# *Chapter Seventeen*

Fighting a fierce headache and a terrible thirst, Luke opened his eyes. Without moving, he looked around and found he was in a bedroom he'd never seen before. It could have been a three-star motel with a dresser, a table and chairs and a door leading to a small bathroom. The entrance door was closed, and there was something funny about the drapes. They were closed tightly and hugged the wall, making him think that perhaps there was no window behind them.

He struggled to hold back a spurt of panic, then calmed a little when he saw Gabriella was lying next to him on the queen-size bed. Her eyes were closed. He wanted to push himself up and wake her, but his muscles weren't cooperating.

Instead, he slid his hand toward hers and touched her fingers as he tried to reach her mind.

*Gabriella, wake up. Gabriella.*

She made a small sound and turned her head toward him.

*Luke.*

*Are you all right?*

He felt her taking a physical inventory. *Not exactly. What happened?*

*Did you feel sick and dizzy at Ms. Goodell's house?*

*Yes.*

*I think Solomon drugged us and took us somewhere.*

*Where? Why?*

*I guess we'll find out,* he answered, twining his fingers with hers, fighting panic. The doctor had taken them captive. That couldn't be good. And he obviously hadn't gotten this room ready on the spur of the moment.

He knew Gabriella had these same thoughts and emotions when she drew in a sharp breath.

*What does he want with us?*

*He was experimenting on our mothers. Experimenting on his clients' kids. But he thought he didn't accomplish anything special. Now he's changed his mind. He wants to find out what he created, but I think it would be a very bad idea to let him find out.*

Gabriella nodded against his shoulder. *He said you were from the clinic, too.*

*Yes. I kept wondering why I came to your mom's plantation looking for a room. I must have somehow been drawn there.* He swallowed again. *To complete myself.*

Her hand tightened on his. *Thank God you did. Otherwise I might have ended up here—on my own.*

Even as she silently said the words, he felt panic rising inside her.

*We have to stay calm,* he soothed, trying to set an example. Too bad his head was still fuzzy. He'd like to be thinking clearly in this situation.

*We have to figure out how to get away,* Gabriella said.

*Yes. But maybe first we have to convince him that we're willing to work with him.*

*How?*

*We'll have to play it by ear,* he answered, wishing he had more information about this place and the doctor. The only thing Luke had learned for sure was that the man wasn't fussy about his methods or his morality.

*Do you think he's eavesdropping on us?* Gabriella asked.

*Probably.*

*Then we shouldn't talk about him.*

Was that the right strategy? He wished he knew, but his brain still wasn't functioning well enough to work through the logic.

"I need a drink," she said aloud, and he decided that it would be better not to remain silent.

"So do I." He untangled his fingers from hers and sat up cautiously. The movement made his head spin, and he waited a moment before easing off the bed, then braced his hand against the night table.

When he felt comfortable in a vertical position, he walked cautiously across the tile floor and into the bathroom, where he found two plastic cups. Not glasses, he noted.

He ran cold water and took a long draft, then brought water to Gabriella. She had pushed herself up and reached for the cup, then drank.

"How do you feel?" he asked.

"Not great."

"Don't get up yet."

He walked to the wall with the draperies and pulled them aside. As he'd guessed, there were only cinder blocks behind them.

"It looks like we're in a basement," he said.

"There aren't many basements in Louisiana. Well, except for the kind at the plantation house."

"Then a room without windows."

"Oh, great." She swallowed and gave him a direct look. "Why are we here, do you think?"

"I wish I knew."

Too restless to settle, he walked around, opening drawers in the dresser, and found clothing that looked as if it would fit them. He also started looking for anything he might use as a weapon. The lamps were bolted down. As far as he could see, the room had nothing that would help them escape.

He was thinking about trying the door when it opened. Dr. Solomon stepped inside. A man with a tranquilizer gun like the one they'd seen earlier was right behind him.

Luke started back toward Gabriella, but Solomon shook his head. "Stay where you are."

Luke stopped in his tracks.

"How are you feeling?" the doctor asked.

"Like I've been hit over the head with a sledgehammer. Thanks so much."

"I'm sorry for the inconvenience," Solomon answered.

Luke snorted. "I'll bet."

The doctor studied them with curious eyes, then turned to the guard. "Step back a few feet. I want to talk to my guests."

The man followed directions, and Solomon walked into the room, then pressed a button on a remote control he was holding. A plastic panel slid into place, blocking the exit but not the gunman's view.

"If you're thinking of trying anything tricky, disabuse yourself of that idea," the doctor said. "The plastic has two purposes. To block the exit and to act as a seal. At the first sign of trouble, I can flood the room with gas. We'll all pass out, of course, but Marvin will bring me out. And you will be punished for your disobedience. Is all that clear?"

Luke swallowed. "You're thinking in very draconian terms."

"At this point, it's my best option." He pulled out one of the chairs at the table and sat down.

Once again, when Luke took a step toward Gabriella, the doctor spoke quickly. "I'd appreciate it if you stay where you can't touch."

"Why?"

"I believe the two of you can communicate mentally when you are touching."

Luke kept his gaze steady. "How did you come to that conclusion?"

"You need to know the background of my old experiments. But let me back up. With the fertilized eggs from my clinic, I was doing microsurgery on blastocytes. As I said, the goal was to produce children with increased intelligence, but I got a normal intelligence distribution among the offspring. Which was disappointing from a scientific point of view."

"Yeah, I'll bet."

"But then that other couple showed up in town asking questions about the clinic. Actually, they weren't the only ones. There was another man and woman. The two couples seemed to have had some kind of psychic battle out in a swampy area."

"What happened?"

"There were no witnesses, but only one couple survived."

"How do you know all this?"

"By direct observation of the battleground and the information I pieced together. There were trees and foliage with burn marks. And we did find some partial human remains in the swamp—chewed by alligators and other creatures."

Luke winced.

"It appears that people with your abilities may not be friendly to each other."

"Why not?"

"Perhaps we can find out."

Luke took that in, longing to cross to Gabriella, but he stayed where he was. And he didn't allow his mind to flick toward hers—lest the doctor have some way of detecting that, too.

"I do have to congratulate you," Solomon said.

"About what?" Luke snapped. He was damn tired of the doctor's condescending attitude. Too bad he couldn't just punch the bastard in the jaw.

"The two of you could be dead. And not from a battle with others of your kind."

Your kind. A nice way to put it. Did that mean the doctor didn't think of them as human? That would be too bad because it would mean they'd sunk to the level of lab rats in Solomon's eyes.

The man was speaking again. "Did you experience any headaches or mental disorientation when you were establishing your mental bond?"

Gabriella spoke up. "Why do you ask?"

"Well, after I found out about those other couples, I started going back through the clinic records, cross-checking to see if anyone else had gotten together. It turns out they had. There were several other couples where the man and woman had been born as the result of clinic procedures. The others were found dead in bed together."

Gabriella sucked in a sharp breath. "That's the truth?"

"Yes."

"But why?"

"They died of cerebral hemorrhages. Somehow the connection between them triggered a buildup of pressure in the brain."

Luke winced, remembering the terrible pain in his head the first times he and Gabriella had touched intimately. It had only stopped when they'd finally made love. Why had they survived? Maybe the others had backed away at the last minute. Or maybe it was what Gabriella had said before. If you didn't trust the other person completely, the connection wouldn't work.

The doctor was studying him intently. "Do you still get a headache when you're intimate?"

"None of your business," he snapped.

"I'm making it my business."

"No," Luke said in a harsh voice. "I mean, the headaches went away."

"I'm glad to hear that." He laughed. "It would be a little inconvenient to get a headache every time you wanted to have sex."

Luke glared at him.

"I was watching you on closed-circuit television when you woke up," Solomon continued. "You didn't speak to each other—which would be the normal situation. Instead, you were holding hands and lying silently on the bed. But I could tell from your expressions that you were having a silent conversation."

*Oh, great,* he couldn't stop himself from projecting toward Gabriella.

*My fault,* she answered.

*Of course not. We were both trying to figure out what to do, but don't reach for me now.*

"Do you have to be touching to communicate that way?" Solomon asked.

"Yes," Luke answered immediately, thinking that the less this guy knew about their talent, the better.

"Well, we can test that later. What else can you do besides speak telepathically?"

"Nothing," Gabriella answered.

The doctor stroked his chin. "After the other couples fought, it looked like they'd been hurling energy bolts out in the bayou. As I said, there was a good deal of tree damage."

"Maybe they have talents we don't have. Or they had a long time to develop them."

"Yes, one of the couples had been together for years," the doctor said. "Apparently they ran into each other in a twelve-step program in Baltimore." He laughed. "From what I can tell, they made their living as scam artists. Do you suppose they were able to influence other peoples' behavior?"

"No idea," Luke snapped, thinking that this guy was a fount of information.

IN A BATTERED SUV SPEEDING toward Houma, Rachel Gregory gasped as she caught some of the conversation between Luke Buckley and Dr. Solomon.

"What?" Jake asked urgently, without taking his gaze from the road.

"Solomon's taken them captive. He knows about the battle we had with Mickey and Tanya."

"How?"

"He was doing research. He knew about couples like us—but who were found dead in bed."

She opened her mind, giving him access to the scene she'd just witnessed. "He's going to do something awful."

Jake clamped his hands on the steering wheel. "Can we get to them in time?"

"I don't know. But it doesn't help that he's made them think that we might be out to kill them."

"Can we send them a message?" Jake asked.

"Not from here. We have to get closer."

"Do we know where to find them?"

"I think he's got some kind of laboratory at the home of a nurse who used to work for him. She's his partner in crime and his mistress, I think."

SOLOMON WAS SPEAKING. "I wanted to see what would happen when you woke up, but I think it would be wise to separate the two of you now so you can't work up anything dangerous." He kept his gaze on Luke as he pressed the remote again. "You will come with me."

As the plastic shield slid open, Luke thought of trying to

attack, but he knew that neither he nor Gabriella were in any shape to take on two men—one of them armed.

Luke turned to see panic written on Gabriella's face.

"It's going to be okay," he said, wondering if he was telling a lie.

She simply stared at him, looking lost and alone. He ached to go to her and take her in his arms, but he knew that would probably earn at least one of them another tranquilizer dart. Struggling to control the anger rising inside him, he followed the doctor out of the room.

Behind him Gabriella was silently screaming, *Luke, Luke,* which made him feel as though he had a knife in his heart.

*I'll come back for you as soon as I can,* he answered, unsure when that would be.

The room had looked as if it might be in a small motel, but the corridor outside was completely utilitarian with cinder-block walls painted green and the vague smell of disinfectant in the air, making Luke wonder what kind of experiments the doctor was doing. Not dissection, he hoped. But with this guy, he wouldn't be surprised if Solomon kept cages of little animals to experiment on—just for fun.

The security guard with the gun stayed behind them as Solomon led the way down the hall to a laboratory. There were banks of computers and the kind of medical equipment he'd seen in emergency rooms.

When Luke's gaze zeroed in on the operating table in one corner, he cringed, but the doctor gestured toward a wooden armchair bolted to the floor.

"Have a seat," Solomon said.

With no other choice, Luke sat. He was trying not to focus on Gabriella, but he was aware of her in the back of his mind.

*He could be using the hidden camera. Don't react to any of this,* Luke told her.

"Put your hands on the chair arms," Solomon ordered matter-of-factly.

When Luke had done as directed, the doctor fastened his wrists to the chair with duct tape. Then he did the same with his ankles.

Luke tested the bonds and knew that he wasn't getting up anytime soon.

HE KEPT HIS GAZE ON THE doctor as the man pivoted away and pulled a cell phone from his pocket, clicked open a line, hunched his shoulders and spoke in a low voice.

Luke struggled to remain impassive as a disturbing scene flashed into his mind: two more tough-looking guards entered the room where Solomon had left Gabriella. She was sitting on the side of the bed and looked up in alarm as they stepped into the room.

"Let's go," one of them said.

"Where?" she asked, struggling to keep her voice steady.

"You'll find out."

*Luke,* she called to him. *Luke.*

*Do what they say. We're not in any shape to protest. Whatever this is, we'll get through it.*

When she stood, one of them used his gun to gesture her out of the room.

As she stepped into the hall and followed the same course he had, he struggled to stay in contact with her. They led her past the room where he was sitting to a similar facility a few doors down.

Again there was a wooden armchair in the center of the space.

"Sit down," one of the men said.

Gabriella sat.

Just as Solomon had done with him, they taped her arms to the chair, then her ankles.

Aware that Solomon was watching him closely, Luke kept his eyes unfocused as though he had no idea what was happening outside this room.

"Now we're going to find out if the two of you are aware of each other," the doctor said as he pushed a button on a console whose screen was hidden from Luke.

He didn't know what was going to happen next, but he knew it wasn't going to be good.

# Chapter Eighteen

One of the men raised his hand and slapped Gabriella across the face. She cried out at the unexpected pain.

She knew that Solomon was watching on a screen in the room down the hall. And she knew Luke had also seen—in his mind. But he sat without moving as though he had no idea what was happening.

She was also aware that Solomon was dividing his attention between the screen and Luke.

"What's going on?" Luke said in an even voice. "What the hell is this all about?"

Solomon ignored him. In the next moment, the doctor raised his hand and slapped Luke across the face so hard that she saw his head whip to the side. He gritted his teeth and glared at the man while sending Gabriella a silent message.

*Do the same thing I did. Don't react. Don't let him know that you can watch me.*

Horror shot through her, but she knew she had to make the men who held her captive think that she didn't know what was going on down the hall. She struggled to sit impassively through Luke's abuse.

In the background, she could hear Solomon talking on a cell phone to one of the men with her, but his voice was too low for her to hear. She kept her vision turned inward, fighting to hide her reaction.

Had they passed the test?

Down the hall, Solomon raised his voice, talking to Luke again.

"I'm not convinced that you don't know about what's happening in the other room."

"What are you talking about?" Luke asked.

"There are two of my guards with your girlfriend. Both men who have no compunctions about torturing a woman. Suppose I have them rape her? To stop them would you let me know that you're in contact with her?"

Luke glared at him. "If you do that, I'll kill you."

The doctor kept his gaze on Luke. "How do you propose to do that?"

Even while she battled not to let her terror show, Gabriella struggled to pretend that she couldn't hear the doctor.

One of the men was talking on the phone again. When he gave her a nasty grin and walked toward her, she cringed, but the chair prevented her from fleeing. Would the doctor really carry out his threat?

She prayed it was just a bluff, even when the sick feeling in the pit of her stomach argued for the worst.

Could she use her mind to stop him? She'd done it before when she was desperate.

Her heart was pounding so hard that it threatened to break through the wall of her chest.

But before the man reached her, she heard an alarm bell ringing.

LUKE HEARD THE SHARP CLANG of an alarm.

Solomon looked up in surprise.

"What the hell is that?" the doctor growled, shooting Luke an angry look.

Luke shrugged. "Your guess is as good as mine."

An intercom buzzed and Violet said, "We have another visitor."

"Let me see who it is."

He walked to a computer monitor.

Luke saw on the screen a car stop in the parking lot. A tall, white-haired man, possibly in his seventies, climbed out. He walked with a springy step toward the main door of the laboratory.

Luke stared at him. He was familiar. Had he seen him before?

Then it came to him. It must be Bill Wellington. He'd been wearing a disguise when he'd killed George, but he couldn't disguise his walk or his aggressive manner.

He strolled toward a one-story, solidly built building, much like a warehouse. That must be where Luke and Gabriella were.

"Wait right there," the doctor called out over his shoulder with an ironic note in his voice as he hurried toward the door.

*Not if I can help it.*

The doctor stepped into the hall. Once he was out of the room, the lock clicked, but at least Luke was alone.

*Thank God,* Luke silently shouted to Gabriella. *Are you all right?*

*Yes. But...those men.*

*Don't think about what might have happened. Think that we have a reprieve. A chance to get the hell out of here.*

*Yes. Right. Can we use our minds to escape?*

*I don't know, but we'll be a lot more effective if we're together.*

While he spoke, Luke was tugging on the tape. Unfortunately, there were too many layers for him to have an effect.

*We almost started a fire in the cabin. Could we use heat to stretch the tape?* Gabriella asked.

*Yeah. Good idea, but don't burn yourself. See if you can warm up the tape or soften it so you can pull your hands free. I think I'm doing it,* he added as he felt the bond begin to give a little. How long would it take to loosen them enough for him to escape?

While he worked, he sent Gabriella another message. *That alarm announced that someone had arrived. I'm almost sure it's Bill Wellington. But he doesn't look quite the same. Different cheekbones. Eyebrows. He must have been wearing heavy makeup when he captured George.*

SOLOMON BARKED ORDERS as he strode down the hall. "Marvin, you're with me. Carl, stay at the security station."

Moments later, he and his most lethal-looking guard stepped into the reception area. Violet was waiting for him, alarm registering on her face.

He switched on another monitor, giving her a view of the parking area.

The white-haired man had reached the front door where he pushed the buzzer and waited.

Violet gasped. "It's Wellington, isn't it? Don't let him in."

"I think that would be a mistake." He buzzed the visitor through.

Wellington strolled in the door as though he owned the place. Thirty years had passed, but there was no mistaking the intruder's glittering eyes and determined mouth.

"Hold it right there," the doctor said, raising the gun in his hand. The guard beside him did the same.

The newcomer stopped and eyed the three of them with interest.

"What the hell are you doing here?" Solomon demanded, keeping his voice steady but with difficulty.

Instead of answering the question, the visitor said, "I

see you didn't curtail your activities when I had your clinic burned down."

"Why should I? It's a free country. And I see you didn't quit the cloak and dagger stuff when you disappeared from sight and changed your name."

"No. Don't play games with me. I've monitored your emails. I know you're still doing research. Using illegal aliens for guinea pigs. A lot of them have died testing your AIDS vaccine."

"I'll make a fortune when I get it perfected. And if you're thinking of trying something tricky, we're not alone here. I have an army of armed men watching us on close circuit," Solomon said, wondering how many men constituted an army.

"I'm not here to start a fight with you."

"Then what?"

"You made plenty of money with your fertility clinic."

Solomon sniffed. "So what? I earned it. Hundreds of couples had children as a result of my treatments. They were way ahead of their time."

"Granted. And they paid off. You used the money to outfit this place."

"I used the money to my advantage. Get to the point. You're not entitled to a cut after all these years."

"I thought your brain experiments came to nothing. It seems that you created something interesting after all."

"Which is?"

"Adults with psychic powers. Which makes them dangerous."

"They have to be touching to activate their powers."

"I wouldn't be so sure of that."

"I was testing two of them when you interrupted. First the man, then the woman. Neither one of them blinked when I tortured the other."

"It could have been their determination not to let you know what they can do."

"We can find out."

Luke had just freed his hands when a voice zinged into his head.

*Luke Buckley. And Gabriella Boudreaux?*

He felt Gabriella gasp.

*Who is that?*

*My name is Rachel Gregory. Jake Harper is with me.*

Gabriella made a sharp sound. *Dr. Solomon asked us about you.*

Now it was Rachel who registered alarm. *What did he ask?*

*If we knew you. He said...* Before Luke could stop her, she went on. *He said you fought another couple with psychic powers. Using thunderbolts or something.*

*Yes, because they tried to kill us,* Rachel answered. *It was either us or them.*

*Why would they attack you?*

*We were hoping they could be friends with us, but they saw us as mortal enemies. Or rather she did. She was power mad and couldn't stand the idea of sharing her special gift with anyone else.*

*And you don't feel that way?* Luke asked.

*No.*

*Why should we believe you?*

*You don't have to, but we're risking our lives to come here and help you get out of this place.*

*Thank you,* Gabriella answered.

*Why do you want to help us?* Luke pressed.

Jake answered, *Because we want to be free of Dr. Solomon—and the other guy. The Badger. I think we can do that together.*

*Okay,* Luke replied, recognizing the other man's pragmatism. If these people were going to attack them later, they'd deal with it.

*Right now Solomon is busy with a visitor. It's the Badger, or Bill Wellington, as he calls himself. He's dangerous. He sent a guy to capture Gabriella, and when his operative failed, Wellington shot him.*

Rachel winced. *We saw him drive in, but we didn't know who he was.*

As they'd been talking, Luke had been working on his bonds. He'd already freed his hands. He pulled the last of the tape off his legs, stood and hurried to the door. It was locked, but he twisted the knob hard, and it gave.

The hall was empty, and he dashed to the room where Gabriella was just freeing her legs.

She stood and came into his arms.

*What should we do?* she asked the other two psychics.

*I believe we can destroy this place. And Solomon and the Badger with it,* Rachel answered.

*If you're thinking about using those thunderbolts the doctor mentioned, let's not forget that we're in here, too.*

*We won't,* Jake Harper answered.

*How did you learn to use thunderbolts?*

*We found out about them when the other couple—Mickey and Tanya—tried to kill us.*

*We had time to practice the skill,* Jake said. *What can you do?*

*We got the guard at a morgue to think we were FBI agents,* Gabriella answered.

*And we just got free of our duct tape bonds by heating the tape,* Luke added.

*Useful,* Jake answered.

When Gabriella gasped, he tensed. *What?*

*They're both coming back. Solomon and Wellington.*

# *Chapter Nineteen*

Luke grabbed Gabriella's hand. *Over here.*

He hurried her toward a storage closet at the back of the room. They darted inside, and he pulled the door shut just before the hall door opened and two sets of footsteps stopped short.

"She's gone!" Solomon shouted.

"See if the man's missing, too."

In the darkness of the storage closet, Luke listened to the two men race out of the room. Had they left the door open?

Gabriella clamped her fingers onto his hand. *Stay here.*

He could still hear the other man and woman, Jake and Rachel, in his head.

*What happened?*

*Solomon came back looking for us. Wellington is with him. We're hiding in a storage closet.*

*Does the lab have a security system?* Jake asked.

*Yes.*

*Can you disable the system in that room? Otherwise they'll have live shots of where you've gone.*

Luke swore under his breath. Could they?

*I think so,* Gabriella answered. To Luke, she said, *but I need to see it.*

He clenched his fists, hating their choices. His pulse pounding, he eased the door open, feeling Gabriella press forward. She looked around the room, trying to locate the video camera.

"Up there," Luke whispered as he pointed to the corner of the room.

"Will shorting out the camera do it?"

"Maybe we can use the one in here to short out the whole system."

She stayed in the doorway, focusing on the camera, and he directed energy toward her. Just as she sent a death ray to the device, he heard footsteps in the hall and pulled her back, easing the closet door closed.

Gabriella gripped his arm, and he knew she was still visualizing the camera and pouring destructive energy into it.

"They're not in either room," the doctor said. "Where the hell did they go?"

"You check the surveillance system. Rewind the tapes from the past fifteen minutes, and I'll check out this room," Wellington said.

One set of footsteps left and Luke heard the other man moving around outside their hiding place.

Gabriella's attention shifted away from the video equipment. There's nobody in here, she shouted with her mind. There's nobody in here.

Could that possibly work? Luke helped her project the message as he scrambled for alternatives.

The closet was five feet deep and ten feet wide with a double row of shelving inside. He took her hand, easing along the front set of shelves, trying to put a barrier between them and the entrance. But they'd only moved a few feet when the door was snatched open, and Wellington appeared with a gun in his hand.

At least they weren't in his direct line of sight.

Luke froze in place, mentally shouting the message, *There's nobody in here. There's nobody in here.*

Luke's stomach clenched. He watched the man's face as his gaze swept the closet, passing them and coming back, then moving on again. He looked perplexed.

*There's nobody in here. There's nobody in here.*

Wellington stayed where he was for a few more seconds, then backed out. When he closed the door, Luke allowed the air in his lungs to trickle out.

*We did it,* Gabriella whispered.

*But how long will it hold? Remember that guy at the hospital.*

Out in the main room, the door opened again and Solomon's angry voice rang out. "The surveillance system is fried."

"Has it ever failed before?" the Badger asked sharply.

"No."

"They must have done it."

"How?"

"With their minds, you moron," Wellington snapped. "I told you they were dangerous."

"What are you saying? That's impossible."

Wellington scoffed. "They're obviously a lot more talented than you thought. I'm glad I arrived in time to save your sorry butt. Stop with this crap about experimenting on them. Shoot to kill. And when we've taken care of this pair, we'll go after the rest of the vipers."

Luke felt a shudder go through Gabriella. *It's going to be okay,* he told her, even when he prayed that it was true.

"That's hundreds of people," Solomon gasped.

"Too bad you were so successful with your nutball project."

"You were excited about using it to extend American exceptionalism."

"And look where it got you."

"You obviously don't understand scientific curiosity."

Wellington's voice turned to ice. "Not by your warped standards."

"You call *me* warped? You're talking about killing a lot of innocent people."

"People who could do who knows what."

When Solomon started to speak again, Wellington cut him off. "We had better stop arguing and find them."

The men hurried out of the room, and Gabriella sagged against Luke.

*What are we going to do?* she asked. *We have to get out of here, but I don't think we can make ourselves invisible to everyone in this building.*

He looked behind them. *No, but we can burn a hole in the wall and get out that way.*

*We've never done anything like that.*

*We have to try.*

The woman who had been talking to them joined the conversation. *We'll help.*

*Do you know where we are?*

*No. But if you start attacking the wall, we'll pick up where you're directing the energy.*

*Okay.* Luke wondered if his desperate suggestion would really work. But he couldn't come up with an alternative.

In the darkness, he and Gabriella eased to the back of the closet, then turned to face the cinder blocks. He ran his hand along the rough surface, and he knew she was following his thoughts.

*Do these things even burn?* she asked.

"With enough heat," he muttered, hoping it was true.

"Which one of us directs it?" Gabriella asked.

"You. We'll do what we did in the cabin." He moved behind her, clasping his arms around her middle as she turned to face the wall. He could feel her trembling in his arms, feel her hesitation.

*Do it,* he whispered in her mind.

He felt her focus on the wall, felt her struggling to generate heat, even as he caught her uncertainty. Should they switch roles?

He knew she heard the question. Knew it strengthened her resolve. She set her mind to the task, and he saw light hit a spot on the wall a little to their right. When the light glowed more brightly, he closed his eyes.

*Got it!* the woman outside the building called out. *We'll work from here.*

Luke slitted his eyes, watching a small hole appear. It was as if the cinder blocks were melting. But at the same time, acrid smoke rose from the place where Gabriella was directing the energy.

She coughed and lost her focus for a moment, then clamped her teeth together and redoubled her efforts while he sent her more energy.

The smoke billowed higher. Suddenly a bell began to ring. Like what had happened when Wellington arrived, only this time Luke knew it was the fire alarm.

Outside, he could hear the guy named Jake Harper cursing. *Now what the hell are we going to do?*

*Give me more energy,* his partner demanded.

Luke did the same, funneling more power to Gabriella. He could see a hole in the wall about the size of a jar top now, daylight on the other side.

He struggled not to cough as the smoke enveloped them. Was the damn stuff toxic?

*Get down,* he told Gabriella, pulling her toward the floor.

They crouched on the cold cement as the hole slowly enlarged. Some of the smoke poured out, but the opening was nowhere big enough for them to get through.

He wanted to tear at the damn thing with his fingers, but he knew he'd only get burned. Looking wildly around, he spotted a metal bar. Just as he began to hack at the wall, the door in back of them flew open.

It was Wellington, a gun in his hand. "Got ya!"

Luke's only option was to push at the shelves behind them, toppling the heavy unit. Boxes and plastic containers flew off as the shelves hit the man, sending him sprawling as the gun in his hand discharged.

"Keep working," Luke shouted to Gabriella. "Get out when the hole's large enough."

"What about you?"

"I'll follow." He leaped up on the shelves, tramping down on them, trying to crush the man who had started all this.

Wellington screamed, but he was still trying to get his gun into firing position.

Out in the room, the sprinkler system had activated, and water was pouring down. The deluge gave Wellington the opportunity to crawl out from under the shelves. Luke went after him, scrambling to grab the weapon. He almost had it, but it slipped out of his hand.

Behind him he heard a cracking sound and knew that the wall was coming apart.

Good. Gabriella should be able to get out, even if he didn't make it.

*Go,* he shouted as he grappled with Wellington on the floor. *Go.*

The man might be old, but he was in fantastic shape, and Luke was still recovering from the effects of the sedative and getting shot a few days earlier. Before he could get the gun, Solomon and an armed man dashed into the room.

"Freeze," the doctor shouted.

Luke twisted around, pulling Wellington on top of himself, using the older man for a shield.

"Hold it right there," Solomon ordered.

Luke and Wellington went still.

The doctor studied them. "Where's the woman?"

Luke raised his chin. "She got away."

"For now. And you didn't," the doctor pointed out in a hard voice. His eyes narrowed. "It looks like we can take care of two problems at the same time. Shoot them both."

# Chapter Twenty

"No!" the Badger shouted. "We're on the same team."

"The same team? Hardly. I thought I was rid of you years ago. You burned my clinic down. Now you come marching back in here giving me orders."

"You don't know what you're doing. You have no idea how to handle these people."

"I'll find out—in my own way." Raising his gun, he aimed at his former associate's head.

Wellington was still pleading, the way George had pleaded, when Solomon pulled the trigger. The bullet hit its mark, sending blood and brain tissue flying.

The doctor turned his attention to Luke. "You're next."

For damn sure he wasn't going to beg for his life. But could he use his power to stop the man from executing him?

*You don't want to shoot Luke Buckley. You don't want to shoot Luke Buckley. You can use him. You can use Luke Buckley.*

The doctor hesitated. Blinking, he stared at Luke.

"What?"

"Maybe you'll find me useful."

"How?"

"I guess we'll have to do some experimenting."

While he spoke, he kept broadcasting the message. *You don't want to kill Luke Buckley. You can use him.*

"We didn't have much time to explore your talents. What can you really do?"

Now what? If he told the truth, maybe the doctor would think he was too dangerous.

"I'd prefer not to discuss it with a couple of guns pointed at me," Luke answered, wondering if he had a chance of disarming the doctor and his security man.

Solomon seemed to be considering the suggestion. Then his face hardened. "Too dangerous."

Luke kept frantically projecting his message. *You don't want to kill Luke Buckley. You can use him.* But the message wasn't having the desired effect.

"You're making my brain feel weird," Solomon muttered.

As the doctor raised the gun, something else happened. One moment, Luke knew he was done for. In the next, Solomon and his guard jerked backward as though they had been caught by an invisible tsunami. They gasped as they flew across the room and slammed into the wall.

With the two men temporarily disabled, Luke took the opportunity to duck back, making for the closet. Before he reached it, he almost ran into Gabriella, who was charging through the door, accompanied by a dark-haired man and woman.

Rachael Gregory and Jake Harper.

They were holding hands with Gabriella as they focused on the doctor and his armed guard.

Luke saw the concentration on Gabriella's face. Seconds later, bolts of energy shot toward the doctor and the guard.

They screamed. Both of them tried to scramble up, but their legs shot out from under them and they fell in a heap in the doorway.

Teeth gritted, Solomon swung around, the gun still in his hand. When he tried to raise the weapon, he screamed and dropped it as though it had suddenly become red hot.

Luke had leaped to join his rescuers, reaching for Gabriella's hand. Instinctively, he added his power to the joint force of the attack. He felt energy surge through the other couple, himself and Gabriella.

As Solomon lay on the floor, he frantically scrabbled in his pocket.

Moments later, he and the guard went still.

"It's over," Jake Harper said, relieved.

"Thank God," Gabriella breathed.

"Let's get out of here," Rachel said. "Hurry," she added, a note of alarm creeping into her voice.

They were just heading toward the closet when Luke felt the whole building shudder, and he flashed back to the moment when the doctor had reached into his pocket.

"Solomon triggered something," Luke shouted.

As the building shook violently, Gabriella screamed, and Luke tried to pull her into his arms, knowing in that instant that they were all going to die. But she kept her hold on Rachel's hand.

Time seemed to slow down so that each second stretched to the breaking point, making the agony of waiting for the end so much worse.

He was bracing for oblivion when he caught a glimmer of hope. Rachel was projecting an image to them of an enormous shimmering soap bubble. No, something far more substantial than a bubble. More like a plastic dome enclosing the four of them, shielding them from the explosion.

A force field, for want of a better name. They crowded together, hands clasped, shoulders pressed.

Hope leaped inside Luke.

Maybe they had a chance after all.

Then he saw that the bubble wasn't entirely stable. When the surface wavered, he knew that it might not hold, and if it disintegrated, they had only postponed death for a few moments.

*Help me,* Rachel shouted as she fought to firm the field.

His heart was pounding as he struggled to hook into her mind and add his own power to the joint effort.

The surface stabilized just before the building disintegrated in a loud clap of thunder. The whole world shook as enormous pieces of building material flew into the air.

Some landed far from where they were standing, but much of the debris rained down on the curved surface surrounding them, striking the transparent skin and bouncing or sliding off.

Luke watched thick clouds of choking dust swirling outside the protective shell. Gradually the particles began to settle and he saw that the whole building had disappeared. He stared at the house where the doctor had drugged them. It had also taken a hit and most of the upper story and the back wall were gone.

"Did we slow down time?" Gabriella gasped out.

"I think so," Jake answered.

"What about the guards and Violet?" Gabriella asked.

"If they were in here, they're dead," Jake Harper answered. "I guess they didn't realize that the doctor had a suicide plan in case things didn't go his way."

"Yeah," Luke answered. "But we always knew he was warped, and now we'd better get the hell out of here before the authorities come to investigate."

As they staggered away, Luke was hardly able to believe what he was seeing, but he knew he and Gabriella had come through a nightmare. He'd wondered if they would survive. Now they stood together in the middle of terrible destruction.

Her thoughts were the same as his. She dropped Rachel's hand and held out her arms. He reached for her and they came together, clinging. When she lifted her face, he lowered his head and their lips met in a fierce kiss that might have gone on forever except that Jake made a throat-clearing sound.

"You're forgetting we've got to get out of here."

Luke struggled to pull himself back to reality. "Right."

"Where's your car?" Jake asked.

Still trying to orient himself, Luke looked around and found what must be the parking lot. Several vehicles had been squashed and dented by debris, including his.

"Wait." Luke walked over and pulled the electrical tape off the license plates.

When he had pocketed the tape, Jake led the way across a field, into the bayou.

As they disappeared under the shade of the trees, he could hear sirens.

They came to a gravel road through the bayou and followed it around a bend, where a beat-up SUV sat.

"By the way, we weren't really introduced. We're Jake Harper and Rachel Gregory."

"Luke Buckley and Gabriella Boudreaux."

"When did you meet?" Gabriella asked as they kept walking toward the car.

"A month ago," Rachel answered. "We've been hiding out most of the time since then."

"Luke and I have been together for less than a week. Also on the run," Gabriella told them.

"And the moment you touched, you started reading each other's thoughts?" Jake asked.

"Yes," Luke answered. "I assume we're all children from the Solomon clinic."

"Must be," Rachel said.

"Sorry we can't offer you better transportation," Jake apologized, when they reached their battered SUV. "But we've been hiding out and we got this secondhand—cheap."

Rachel laughed. "A real hardship for him. You ought to see his fleet of vehicles in the city."

They all climbed into the car. In the backseat, Luke held Gabriella's hand tightly as Jake started the engine and they headed away from the doctor's lab.

Gabriella leaned into Luke, her eyes closed.

"Is it really over?" she said.

"Let's hope so," Rachel answered from the front seat.

When they were about twenty miles from Houma, Jake turned in at another narrow drive that led to a small but comfortable-looking house tucked among tall cypress trees.

"We've been here for a couple of weeks," he said, "hoping we could figure out some way to disable the Badger. We didn't even know Solomon was alive."

"Not anymore. I mean, neither of them," Luke answered.

They all climbed out, crossed to the house and entered a cozy living room.

"How did you find this place?" Luke asked.

Jake laughed. "Vacation rental. Paid cash."

There were comfortable chairs and couches in the living room. Jake gestured toward the couch, and Luke and Gabriella sat, still unwilling to move away from each other, still marveling that they had escaped from Dr. Solomon's clutches.

Jake and Rachel went to the kitchen area and began getting out food.

"You're probably starving," Rachel said as she set down sour cream dip, chips, raw vegetables and shrimp rémoulade.

Luke blinked. After what they'd been through, he could hardly believe the domestic scene. It was like they were two couples who were getting together for a social evening. Only it was a lot more than that.

"What can I get you to drink?" Jake asked.

"Strong coffee," Luke answered. "I could use the jolt."

"How about a cappuccino?"

"You're kidding, right?"

"You can't expect a restaurateur to subsist on ordinary standard brew." He'd bought a restaurant-quality machine, and he busied himself grinding beans, then foaming milk. "The same for you?" he asked Gabriella.

"Yes, thanks."

Jake turned out four perfect cups, and they all sipped and ate the goodies Rachel had put out.

Gradually Luke felt himself unwinding, but he couldn't entirely relax.

"What's next?" he finally asked.

"For starters, we've got choices again," Jake said.

Gabriella sat forward, looking from Jake to Rachel and back again, bursting with the idea that had been rattling around in her head for days.

"Would you like to invest in a restaurant in Lafayette? With a top chef running the kitchen?" Gabriella asked.

"Sounds interesting. Give me a few more details," Jake said.

She told him about the plantation house, the cottages on the property and her own culinary background.

Luke saw him looking at Rachel and knew he was asking silent questions.

She was the one who spoke. "I was wondering if the four

of us should stick together for a while. Maybe see what kind of joint talents we could develop." She cleared her throat. "Your plantation might be the perfect spot. But I'd want to spend a few days in New Orleans each week, doing my tarot card readings."

"Of course," Gabriella agreed.

"And to add to our to-do list, perhaps we want to look for some of the other children from the clinic?" Luke asked.

"Cautiously," Jake answered. "Remember that Mickey and Tanya attacked us."

"They almost killed Jake," Rachel added

Luke whistled through his teeth. "That must have made it hard for you to contact us—and help us escape."

"Yes, but we had to take the chance when we realized you were in trouble," Rachel said. "And as soon as we got close to you, we knew you're good people. Sensing things about customers has always helped me in my tarot card readings."

Luke nodded, thinking he had the same feelings about Jake and Rachel. He trusted them. Which didn't make it any easier to say, "There's one other problem I need to disclose. Hanging around me could be dangerous."

Gabriella tightened her hold on his hand as he said, "I'm writing a book about New Jersey mobsters. They were after me, too."

"Those were the two other men Solomon shot with the tranq gun?" Jake asked.

"You saw that?"

"Well, Rachel viewed the scene remotely." He paused for a second and said, "They're dead. We saw that, too. Which was why we knew how ruthless Dr. Solomon was."

Luke dragged in a breath and let it out. "More wiseguys could come looking for me."

Jake listened to the story of their escape from the apartment in New Orleans, then said, "I think there's an easy solution. Maybe it was already in the back of your mind when you pulled the tape off your plates. Don't you think it's a pretty safe assumption that you got blown up in that explosion? The cops are going to find your car and trace it back to you. We can reinforce the news of your death with some mental misinformation."

"And if anybody asks, you and I separated and I escaped," Gabriella added.

"Then you can come back from the dead when the book's published and the damage is done," Jake said with a laugh.

Luke hoped it would work. For now, it was a good enough solution.

He looked up to see the other couple exchanging silent information.

Rachel stood. "And now that we don't have to hide out from the Badger, I'd like to do some shopping without having to look over my shoulder."

"And I need to contact my restaurant manager," Jake added, "and let him know I'm alive and well."

"You probably want to unwind. Let me show you the guest bedroom," Rachel said. She got up and walked down a short hall. "Make this your home. We'll be gone for a couple of hours."

Before Luke or Gabriella could respond, their new friends had left.

"I guess they knew we wanted to be alone," Gabriella murmured.

*Yeah. She said she was intuitive.* He laughed. "Or she was reading our expressions."

*Oh, Luke.* She reached for him, and he came into her arms. They held each other tightly.

*Did you ever in your wildest dreams think things would work out this way?* she asked.

*No. But I hoped.*

They clung together, and when she raised her face to his, he brought his mouth down for a passionate kiss. A leisurely kiss. As he lifted his head, he said, "Now maybe I can ask you to marry me."

"Maybe?"

He gave her a serious look. "I knew I had to hide out from the mob. And I wasn't going to put you in danger."

"And I wasn't going to let you ditch me."

"Ditch you? I wouldn't put it that way."

"Let's not waste time arguing about it. Are you going to ask me?"

His expression turned serious. "Gabriella Boudreaux, will you marry me?"

"Oh, yes."

She sealed the answer with another kiss as they swayed together in the middle of the room.

"Do you think Jake will go in with me on the restaurant idea?" she asked.

"When he reads your reviews, he'll jump at the chance to back you. And he's got the expertise to make it work."

"I feel so blessed. And not just about my career. I never thought I'd get close to anyone, I mean really close."

"I know."

"Now I have you. And we have them, too. People who understand where we came from—and how precious our life is now."

As he said it, he felt overwhelmed by happiness and the way they had conquered their problems.

*There will always be problems,* Gabriella said. *Like, will our children inherit our special talents?*

*You're already thinking about children?*

*I can't help it.*

He gathered her to him. *But we'll wait awhile, right?*

*Yes. Until we have a better idea of how our lives will work out. But we don't have to worry about the future now. We just have to celebrate what we've earned.*

He linked his hand with hers and led her to the bedroom, intent on showing her how much she meant to him.

* * * * *

# INTRIGUE...

BREATHTAKING ROMANTIC SUSPENSE

## My wish list for next month's titles...

In stores from 18th May 2012:

- ❑ A Daughter's Perfect Secret – Kimberly Van Meter
- & Lawman Lover – Lisa Childs
- ❑ Operation Midnight – Justine Davis
- & A Wanted Man – Alana Matthews
- ❑ High-Stakes Affair – Gail Barrett
- & Deadly Reckoning – Elle James
- ❑ Cowboy's Triplet Trouble – Carla Cassidy

Available at WHSmith, Tesco, Asda, Eason, Amazon and Apple

### Just can't wait?

Visit us Online

You can buy our books online a month before they hit the shops! **www.millsandboon.co.uk**

0512/46

# Special Offers

Every month we put together collections and longer reads written by your favourite authors.

Here are some of next month's highlights—and don't miss our fabulous discount online!

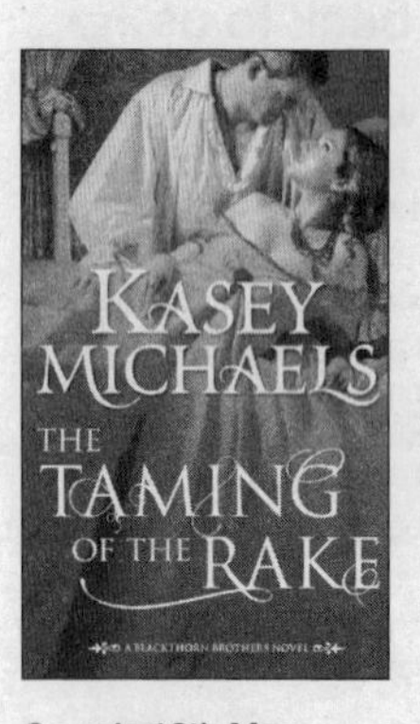


**On sale 18th May**

**On sale 1st June**

**On sale 1st June**

Find out more at
**www.millsandboon.co.uk/specialreleases**

*Visit us Online*

0512/ST/MB375